'I don't deny it

'You have always b[...]
you, Matthew, but [...]
stupid enough to let you take advantage of the
fact!'

He laughed harshly. 'Do you think that you can
just turn your feelings on and off at will? No,
Maggie. When you lie in bed tonight your body
will ache for my touch, your blood stir waiting
for the fire only I can ignite.'

Dear Reader

In this year of European unity, July sees the launch in hardback (September paperback) of an intriguing new series—contemporary romances by your favourite Mills & Boon authors, but with a distinctly European flavour. Look out for the special cover of a love story every month set in one of the twelve EC countries, which will take you on a fascinating journey to see the sights, life and romance, Continental style.

Vive l'amour in 1992—who do *you* think is Europe's sexiest hero?

The Editor

Jennifer Taylor was born in Liverpool, England, and still lives in the north-west, several miles outside the city. Books have always been a passion of hers, so it seemed natural to choose a career in librarianship, a wise decision as the library was where she met her husband, Bill. Twenty years and two children later, they are still happily married, she is still working in the library, with the added bonus that she has discovered how challenging and enjoyable writing romantic fiction can be!

Recent titles by the same author:

GUILTY OF LOVE
LOVE IS A RISK

OLD LOVE,
NEW LOVE

BY
JENNIFER TAYLOR

MILLS & BOON LIMITED
ETON HOUSE   18-24 PARADISE ROAD
RICHMOND   SURREY   TW9 1SR

*First published in Great Britain 1992
by Mills & Boon Limited*

© Jennifer Taylor 1992

*Australian copyright 1992
Philippine copyright 1992
This edition 1992*

ISBN 0 263 77651 4

*Set in Times Roman 11 on 12 pt.
01-9208-50149 C*

Made and printed in Great Britain

CHAPTER ONE

IT HAD been three years since she'd seen him, three years which faded into nothing when she looked up and found him watching her across the room. Just for a moment she held his gaze, then lowered her eyes, feeling her heart pounding and perspiration breaking out all over her body. She'd thought he was still in America, so what was he doing here? Why had fate suddenly decided that their paths should cross when she was just getting over him?

'Maggie.'

She had no need to turn her head to know that it was him standing next to her. How many times had she heard him say her name in that same deep, steady voice? How many times had she lain awake with tears on her face, listening to the echo of it in her head? Over the past three years she must have heard the memory of those deep tones a thousand times or more, yet she couldn't help the shudder which ran through her body as she heard them now.

'Are you all right? You look...well, shaken almost.'

She looked up then, pinning a smile to her lips, her green eyes bright as glass as they met his. 'Of course I'm all right. Why shouldn't I be? How are you, Matthew?'

'Well, thanks.'

'Good. I didn't know that you were back in England. Are you here on holiday?'

'No, I've come back to live here.' He shrugged slightly, his eyes lingering on the soft curves of her face before moving on to the richness of her hair where it lay in heavy waves against the black fabric of her dress. 'I got tired of living at such a hectic pace, so I decided it was time to come back.'

'I see.' She forced herself to smile brightly at him, fighting against the faintness which threatened to claim her at the news. She had been dreading this moment, praying that it would never happen, that he would decide to stay in America for good, but it seemed that all her prayers had gone unanswered, and she was suddenly afraid. If he ever found out then . . .

She forced the thought from her mind, terrified that he would somehow know what she was thinking as he'd done so many times before. She couldn't let him find out, *wouldn't* give him the chance to hurt her again as he'd hurt her before. Whatever it took, she would keep him out of her life, because there was no way she was going through all that pain again.

Picking up her glass, she drained the last of the wine then set it back down on the table, making herself act as naturally as possible. Matthew was clever, far too clever to miss any signs if she was careless. She had to hide her fear, her eagerness to get away from him, otherwise she would arouse his suspicions. Thank heavens that no one knew her here at the party apart from Marie. She'd only come tonight at her friend's insistence, but she would easily be able to make her promise not to tell anyone where she lived. The one thing she didn't want was for Matthew to turn up at the house.

Her hand shook as she picked up the small black satin evening bag from the table and slipped it under her arm, but she fought against the attack of nerves, knowing she had to brazen it out.

'Well, it's been good seeing you again, Matt, but I'm afraid I really have to leave now.'

He raised a mocking dark brow, pushing back an immaculate cuff to glance at the expensive watch on his wrist. 'So early? Doesn't sound like the Maggie I used to know.'

Her teeth clamped together until her jaws began to ache as she held back the sharp retort. She couldn't afford to retaliate, couldn't set a match to that anger which always seemed to ignite so easily when they were together. She had to play everything cool and calm, keep things moving on an even keel, untainted by the fiery passions she could sense even now burning beneath the surface. 'I have to be up early tomorrow. I'm working in the morning.'

His eyes narrowed as he slid a glance over her slender figure in the clinging black dress, a faintly contemptuous curl to his lips. 'You're still modelling, then?'

'Of course. What else would I be doing?' She kept her tone light, fighting the hot surge of anger which rose in her breast. He had always hated what she did for a living, always treated it with that same mocking contempt, but if it hadn't been for her modelling then she would have found it hard to manage these past few years. True, she no longer did the high-fashion shows which could take her out of the country for days at a time at short notice, but at least she made a comfortable living from the mail-order catalogues and magazines she was in such demand for.

Anxious to put an end to the conversation, she held her hand out in a stiffly polite gesture, then immediately wished she hadn't when his fingers closed round hers. Sensation rippled through her in hot waves, taking her back in time so that she felt dizzy with the speed of it.

'Maggie.'

His voice was no more than a whisper that barely broke through the noisy hum of voices all around them, but she heard every syllable, *felt* every nuance touching her skin. His fingers tightened and he drew her closer, bringing her body into contact with his so that she could feel the warmth of his hard flesh, smell the familiar heady aroma of his skin. Suddenly she was drowning in sensation, her head filling with wave after wave of memory, and she wrenched her hand away as she struggled to surface.

'I have to go. I'm sorry, Matt, but I——'

'You can't fight it, Maggie. It's still there between us, no matter how hard you try to deny it.'

There was a hard assurance in his voice, a steely certainty in his eyes as they slid over her face, and suddenly Maggie was consumed with anger. How could she have been such a fool as to forget even for a moment what had happened and how he had treated her?

Cold contempt lay starkly on her face as she stared back at him. 'I never did deny it, Matthew. It was you who divorced me . . . remember?'

His face went rigid, every bone outlined under the lean flesh, hot colour rimming his angular cheekbones before he made an obvious effort to relax and smiled that knowing smile she'd grown to hate so much. 'Oh, I remember, Maggie. I remember everything, but it's not over yet.' He reached out to lift a strand of her hair and twine it round his fingers, studying the way it lay like a circle of fire against his skin. 'It won't be over until I decide that it is.'

His arrogance took her breath away. She stepped back, feeling the painful tug on her scalp as she pulled her hair free from his grasp. 'Until you decide? Well, it seems to me that you made your decision three years ago! Or have you suddenly realised that you were wrong?' She laughed, a bitter little sound, her face paper-white, her eyes a brilliant emerald in contrast. 'What a turn-up for the books that would be, the great Matthew Kane actually admitting he'd been wrong!'

His smile faded, his face filling with contempt. 'I made no mistake, Maggie. Everything I said was true then, and I don't see any reason to change it now!'

What had she really expected? That he would admit he'd been wrong, actually come out and say the words which three years ago she would have sold her soul to the devil to hear him say? The utter futility of it all left her suddenly drained, and she turned away, pushing her way through the crowd of people, ignoring the curious glances from those close enough to have heard the exchange. In a trance, she made her way to the cloakroom and found her coat, shivering as she drew it on and felt the cold satin lining slither over her skin.

'How are you getting home?'

She hadn't realised he had followed her, and now she started violently, stepping back as he came towards her, her eyes widening in alarm.

'For heaven's sake, Maggie, what's wrong with you? Why are you acting like this? I know we didn't part on the best of terms, but is that any reason to act as though you think I'm going to beat you?'

She drew in a shaky breath, willing herself to stay calm and control the mounting hysteria she could feel writhing in her stomach. She was acting like a fool, making him suspicious, and that was the last thing she must do. Yet it was hard to stop the bitterness from tearing her resolve apart. She had loved this man. Once he had been the very centre of her world, and he had repaid that love in the cruellest way possible. There was no way she could forget that now, or ever.

'No, you never did that, did you, Matthew? You never laid a finger on me, but then you never had to. You had your own very special way of punishing me which was far more effective!'

He stepped back as though she had struck him, his face under the tan going white with anger. 'Can you blame me? What man wouldn't want to punish you after what you did?' He laughed, a harsh, ugly sound which made a shudder run through her when she heard it. 'You tell me, Maggie, dearest, what man would calmly turn the other cheek when he found out he'd been played for a fool and that his wife was sleeping with his brother?'

It was the same accusation now as before and it shouldn't have hurt. Three years and so much distance between them should have eased the pain of hearing those words, but it didn't. Every word felt like a knife ripping into her heart, tearing it apart, leaving her as open and wounded as she'd been before. Just for a moment Maggie stared at him, everything she felt showing on her face, then abruptly she turned on her heel and ran out of the door.

'Maggie! Dammit, Maggie, come back here at once!'

The angry order echoed after her as she ran down the steps and into the street, but she didn't stop. She had to get away, had to run from Matthew, had to run from the pain again. Half blinded by tears, she raced between the cars parked along the kerb, barely aware of the abusive screech of a horn when a taxi slewed to a halt to avoid hitting her as she ran into its path. Her hands were shaking so hard that she couldn't seem to fit the key into the lock of her car, but at last she managed it and scrambled inside, snapping the lock down behind her, terrified that Matthew would try and drag her out again. She glanced round, searching the dark street for his tall figure, then let out a shuddering sob of relief when she saw him standing on the steps of the house, making no attempt to follow her.

Flicking on the engine, she gunned the car to life, then set off, the tyres screeching as she pulled away from the kerb far too fast. There was a moment as she drew level with the house when she couldn't help but look towards the door, but he had gone, the doorway empty, light spilling across the pavement in rich golden pools, and bitterness touched her face.

She'd been a fool to run away like that, to act like a hysterical teenager. Matthew Kane didn't give

a damn about her. He would never have deigned
to race after her and make a scene in the middle of
the street. He didn't have to. If he wanted to find
her again then he would do so, and there wouldn't
be a single thing she could do to stop him. Just the
thought terrified her. For three years now she'd
heard not one word from him, so why had he suddenly turned up again? Was it just mere coincidence or a twist of fate that had brought him to
that party tonight? Or was there another far more
sinister reason behind that apparently unexpected
encounter? Surely he couldn't have found out what
she'd gone to such lengths to keep hidden from
him?

She took her time, concentrating on steering the
small car along the network of city streets, terrified
that the shock would affect her judgement, yet it
was barely eleven when she pulled on to the drive
and cut the engine. She sat quite still, her hands
resting limply along the smooth curve of the
steering-wheel, feeling the tremors of shock still
coursing through her body. She had thought that
she was over him, thought that if they ever did meet
again she would be able to handle it with all the
maturity the past three years had given her, but
she'd gone to pieces just as she'd used to do,
crumpled beneath the bitter accusations, the total
assurance that he was right. He had divorced her,
ended their marriage and any commitment they
owed each other, but she wasn't free. She couldn't
be, not when he could affect her so easily with just
a touch, a look, a cruel, devastating word. Yet
somehow she had to pick up the pieces again as

she'd picked them up before and mould them back into the life she'd struggled to build for herself. She wouldn't let Matthew destroy her again.

She sat up, drawing in a quiet breath as she glanced in the mirror to brush the tumbling mass of rich red hair back from her face. She looked paler than usual, her ivory complexion devoid of all colour, her eyes over-bright. She reached for her bag, then stopped, a tiny frown marring her smooth brow when she failed to find it on the passenger-seat. Had she left it behind at the party, put it down in the cloakroom when she'd fetched her coat? She wished she could remember, but it was difficult to think at that moment. With a shrug of resignation she gave it up, settling for pinching her cheeks between thumb and forefinger to bring a touch of colour to them instead of the quick application of blusher she'd been planning on. Apart from her make-up and a few pound coins, there was nothing of value in the bag. She would ring Marie to-morrow and ask her to make enquiries from their hostess if the bag had been found.

She opened the car door and stepped out, squaring her shoulders before walking up the narrow path to the front door and ringing the bell. The wind was blowing up stronger now, shaking the trees and sending the dead autumn leaves skit-tering across the garden in little eddies. She shivered as she waited for the door to be opened. In a few months' time it would be Christmas again, the time of year she'd come to dread. She had to put what had happened tonight behind her, otherwise she would never be able to cope with that as well as all the memories.

'Well, you're back early. I didn't expect you until the early hours. What happened?'

Pulling the door open, David smiled at her, stepping back to let her into the hall. Maggie forced a smile to her lips, walking past him to take off her coat and hang it away in the cloakroom.

'I must be getting old, I think. Parties don't seem to have the appeal they used to have.'

David laughed as he closed the door, crossing his arms across his chest as he ran an openly admiring glance down her trim figure in the clinging black mini dress. 'In that get-up, you look no more than eighteen, so don't give me that. I'm definitely not buying that excuse. Come on, admit it... you just couldn't wait to get back home to my scintillating company.'

Maggie laughed, feeling some of the tension easing out of her at his teasing. Reaching up, she touched her lips to his cheek in a gesture of affection. 'Got it in one. Why do I ever try fooling you?'

He slid an arm round her shoulders, drawing her against him as they walked down the narrow hall and into the small sitting-room. 'Beats me, Magdalena Duncan. You'd think you would have a bit more sense at your age!'

'Cheeky monkey!' Picking up a cushion off one of the chairs, Maggie tossed it at him before sinking down with a weary sigh and kicking off her high black patent shoes. She closed her eyes, letting the peace and warmth of the room seep into her weary body, then opened them abruptly when a picture started to imprint itself behind her lids. She'd thought she was over that too, conjuring up pictures of Matthew every time she closed her eyes, but obviously tonight's encounter had triggered it all off again.

'What is it, Maggie? What's wrong? You look as though you've just seen a ghost, not come from what Marie promised to be the "best party of the season".'

There was open concern in David's voice as he sat down in the chair opposite and studied her, but she shook her head, unwilling to tell him what had happened. David had a stake in the past: his life had been irrevocably altered by what had happened. He, too, had been forced to change course and make fresh plans, learn to live with the pain. It wouldn't be fair to tell him and reopen the wounds when there might be no need.

'Nothing is wrong. I'm just tired, that's all. Has everything been all right, all quiet on the western front, so to speak?' She could tell he didn't believe her, but he let it go, settling back in the chair, swamping it with his big muscular frame. In the soft glow of the nearby lamp his hair gleamed the colour of a new pound coin, his grey eyes steady and level as they met hers, and not for the first time she wished that it could have been David she'd fallen in love with. David, who had held her together these past years, always there when the pain became too much for her to bear on her own. Life would have been so different for all of them if it had been him she'd given her heart to.

'Not a murmur. I don't know what you do to that...' He broke off, grimacing wryly as a thin wail echoed from upstairs. 'It seems I spoke too soon.'

Maggie grinned, glad of the interruption. There was no point sitting there wishing and wanting: lord knew it didn't change anything. 'Psychic, I'd call it. I'll go.'

'No, you stay there. I'll do the honours and earn my supper. Play your cards right and I'll even let you make me a cup of cocoa as a reward!'

'You're on. I'll just go and put some milk on to heat. And, seeing as you've been so good, how about a chocolate biscuit to go with——?' She stopped abruptly, glancing at her watch when the doorbell rang. 'I wonder who that is at this time of night?'

'Want me to go?' David paused in the doorway but she shook her head, pushing him ahead of her along the hall.

'No, I'll get it. It will probably be one of the neighbours, and we don't want to give them anything to start gossiping about. I have my reputation to consider, after all.'

David rolled his eyes, his mouth twisting wryly. 'Heaven forbid that you should be caught with a man in the house at eleven o'clock at night!'

Maggie laughed, waiting until he'd taken the steep stairs two at a time before opening the door, then felt all the laughter drain away in a swift tide as she saw the man standing outside.

'Hello again.'

'What do you want?'

Her voice was hard as she fought for control, and his face tightened in anger. He stepped forward, pushing against the door, but she leant against it, using all of her slight weight to hold it against his entering.

'I asked what you wanted,' she repeated, staring back at him, feeling her heart thudding with a sickening force in her throat. It was like the very worst of her nightmares to find him here, outside her door, but she had to control the fear she could feel racing in dizzying spirals through her. So much depended on her ability to handle this situation.

He seemed to hesitate, his eyes searching hers with an intent scrutiny she remembered so well. Once it had thrilled her to the core, the way he had looked at her as though trying to see right inside her soul; now it terrified her. She drew in a shuddering breath, hating the fact that he *knew* how she felt. Why was he doing this, reawakening memories which must be almost as bitter to him as they were to her? It didn't make any kind of sense, but then, nothing ever had when they were together. Maybe that had been part of the trouble, the fact that their relationship had always been so frenzied, filled with passions of one kind or another. They had never had time to get to know one another as ordinary people.

'You dropped this when you left the party. I thought you might need it.'

She was so wrapped up in her thoughts that she jumped when he spoke, flinching away when he pushed the black satin bag into her hands. He swore roughly, using his superior strength to push the door open and step into the hall, glaring down at her with eyes that were chips of pure blue ice.

'You're doing it again, Maggie, jumping like a startled little rabbit. Is it really so difficult to speak to me in a civilised manner for a few minutes?'

'Yes!' She spat the answer back at him, whirling round, her hands clenched at her sides. 'You give me one good reason why I should act civilised, Matthew, and I'll give you ten others why I shouldn't! Our relationship has never been *civilised*, and you know it. You should do, because you're the one who brought it down to this level!'

'I brought it down? You have the audacity to blame me?' He didn't raise his voice; if anything, it dropped even lower, the words almost gentle, yet there was nothing gentle about the stark anger on his face, nothing gentle about the hands which reached out and gripped her arms. 'You were the one who brought it all down to gutter-level! You were the one who couldn't live without the attention you were used to getting! *You* brought it all on yourself because you can't bear not to have every man you meet dancing attendance on you!'

'No!'

She pressed her hands over her ears, blotting out the cruel words uttered in that devastatingly gentle way, but he just laughed and dragged her hands down.

'Don't you like hearing the truth, sweet Maggie? Does it offend your delicate ears to hear what I think of you——?'

'Let her go, Matthew. You've said quite enough.'

No! The denial echoed in her head even as she looked past the man who was holding her and saw David standing halfway down the stairs. Just for a moment the whole scene seemed to crystallise, the action suspended, the players frozen in time. It was only when Matthew started to turn that she came to her senses.

She pushed past him, running towards the stairs, trying to get there before he could look and see what she'd kept secret from him these past three years, but there was no way she could do that now. No way she could turn back the clock and make time stop.

'Well, well, what a touching little scene. You must forgive me if I appear surprised. No one told me, you see, but then, they wouldn't, would they? Not when I've made it plain how I feel about you both. You must forgive me for intruding on you, Maggie. I never realised what a homely little setting this was: my ex-wife, my brother... and their child!'

Her breath caught so tight that for a moment she couldn't breathe, and the whole room started to tilt as she went dizzy through lack of oxygen.

'Maggie! Are you OK?'

David came the rest of the way down the stairs, and shook her slightly, his face etched into lines of concern, and gradually the spasm passed. Slowly Maggie turned her head and looked at the tall dark-haired man across the room before looking back at David and the child he held in his arms. In the bright glare of the overhead light the resemblance was so clear, so sharp, that a person would have to be blind not to see it, but then, Matthew *was* blind: blind with anger, blind with bitterness, blind with that consuming jealousy which had eaten away at their marriage until it had become nothing more than a shell.

Reaching out, she lifted the little girl into her arms, nestling the dark head against her neck as she smoothed a hand over the soft damp curls. For three years she had guarded her secret, lived a life filled with fear that one day he would somehow find out. Yet now he was here, standing just feet away from her, and still he didn't know that the child she held in her arms was his.

It should have been relief she felt at that moment, so why did it feel as though he had just put another wound into her already broken heart?

CHAPTER TWO

'SMILE, darling! You're supposed to be having fun...not attending a funeral.'

Maggie sighed, shaking back the tumbling mass of hair from her face as she spun lightly on her heel then smiled brilliantly into the camera. The whole session had been a nightmare this morning, dragging on and on, and she wished it would come to an end. She didn't feel like standing here posing, dressed in the gaudily bright holiday clothes while inside her head she felt as though every scrap of colour had faded from her life. It was only sheer professionalism that stopped her from walking from the set and going back home to give in to the tears which she'd kept bottled up all night since Matthew had stormed out of the house, his face filled with a bitter contempt which had hurt more than any amount of words. David had wanted to stay with her, of course, worried by the stark pallor of her grief-etched face, but she'd refused. She'd wanted to be alone to lick her wounds and come to terms with what had happened, but that had been impossible. She had stood for hour after hour, staring down at Janey as she'd slept in her cot, and known that she would never come to terms with Matthew's blindness to the truth.

She had thought that the worst thing that could ever happen would be that he would find out about the child, but now she knew that she'd been wrong.

It was the fact that he had seen Janey yet still didn't know that she was his daughter that hurt, and there was no way she would come to terms with that in a hurry.

'Right. I guess that will have to do for today. I don't know what's wrong with you, Maggie, but I would appreciate it if you'd try and sort it out before next week. There's still a lot to get through then, all that summer evening-wear collection for a start, and frankly, at your present showing, I doubt we'll do it!'

Denis's expression was a trifle grim as he wound the film from the camera and put it carefully away into the metal container along with all the others, and Maggie knew that she couldn't blame him for being annoyed. He worked to a tight schedule, and she had been more than a little abstracted all morning, wasting valuable time.

'Yes, of course. Sorry, Denis. I guess I'm a bit tired today.'

He flicked her a glance, stripping the camera off the tripod, working with his customary deftness as he sorted out the valuable equipment. 'And I suppose we have Marie to thank for that. I heard her badgering you into going to that party.'

There was a hard note in his voice which surprised her, and she glanced curiously at him. Denis was one of the easiest photographers she'd ever worked for, not given to outbursts of artistic temperament that so many others she could name indulged in. She had never heard him adopt that tone about anyone, and that he should do so now about Marie, who had always been one of his favourites, surprised her.

He must have caught her look, because his face coloured and he bent over the sturdy metal case, settling the camera and lenses into the heavy foam padding with even more care than usual. All of a sudden Maggie realised what had upset him: *he* had offered to accompany Marie to that party but her friend had laughed off the offer, patting Denis's cheek and murmuring something about not wanting him to spoil her chances of catching herself an eligible male!

So that's the way the wind blew. In a way Maggie wasn't surprised. There had been a lot of undercurrents when Denis and Marie had been together recently, but somehow she'd never put two and two together and realised what was going on. It was more than likely that Marie had been deliberately trying to make Denis jealous by going to the party. If she was then she might come to regret it in the future. No one knew better than Maggie just how destructive jealousy could be in a relationship.

Her face tightened and she turned away, hurrying from the set to undress behind the screens set in the corner of the room. Tossing the bright cottons over the back of the chair, she slid into a pair of slim-fitting denims and a short waist-length dull-green jumper, then creamed the heavy make-up from her face, barely aware of what she was doing as the memories came rushing back. She had tried so hard to forget that brief disastrous year of her marriage, but Matthew's unexpected appearance had chipped away at the barricades she'd built in her mind, letting bits of the past come creeping back, and now it seemed impossible to stop the flow.

They should never have married in the first place. With the benefit of hindsight, she knew that now, but then it had been impossible to see past the passion which had flared so instantly between them. If she had been more experienced then maybe it would all have died a natural death: they would have had an affair and then gone their separate ways once it was over. But she'd been barely eighteen when they had met and completely innocent, and Matthew, with his devastating dark looks and suave assurance, had swept her off her feet.

She had been on an assignment when they had met, modelling jewellery from a top London store at a very exclusive party held for some charity or other. She'd been modelling for just over a year by then and starting to make a name for herself, and had been flattered to be asked to work at the prestigious event along with three other top-flight models. She had been told to mingle with the guests and let them see the jewels close up, and had been enjoying the glitzy occasion when she'd stopped at Matthew's group. She had run through the carefully rehearsed little speech she'd been given then started to move on, when someone had caught her arm and stopped her.

Closing her eyes, Maggie felt a ripple run through her even now as she remembered the touch of those long, lean fingers on her arm. She had stopped immediately, her heart racing, consumed by a heady breathlessness she couldn't understand, and looked straight up into Matthew's eyes. He had held her gaze for a long moment, then slowly reached out and lifted the heavy necklace of gold and diamonds away from her throat, letting his fingers rest in its place against the delicate bones as he'd made a great show of studying the exquisite workmanship, but even in her innocence Maggie knew that it had been the last thing on his mind. He had been as aware of her as she'd been of him, a tingling, heart-stopping awareness which had both shocked and excited her.

When he had finally let the necklace fall back into place she had remained mesmerised for several seconds before turning abruptly away, her movements jerky and uncoordinated, her pulse hammering wildly. All through that long night she had felt him watching her, but he had made no further attempt to detain her again. It was only when she had left the party that she had found him waiting for her outside, his dark hair ruffled by the wind, his blue eyes burning with a fire which had sent answering flames licking along her veins.

In total silence he had held his hand out to her, and she had gone to him, sliding her hand into his, not even feeling surprised when he had bent his dark head and kissed her. His lips had been cool from the night's chill, yet holding a heat which had made her go weak in response. When he had at last raised his head he had studied her face in the pale silvery moonlight filtering through the trees, then reached out and brushed a strand of hair from her cheek in an oddly possessive little gesture which should somehow have warned her of what was to come but which had excited her almost beyond bearing. All she had wanted at that moment *was* to belong to him, yet when she did the belonging had become a nightmare.

'Aren't you ready yet, Maggie?'

She jumped, wrenched from the past by the sound of Denis's voice, and the memories splintered like glass in her mind. She drew in a shaky breath and tossed the used cotton ball into the bin, then stepped from behind the screen, avoiding his rather searching gaze.

'Sure you're all right, love? You don't look quite yourself today.'

She wanted to laugh and cry at the same time, to tell him that no, she wasn't all right, she couldn't be when her life was about to be destroyed yet again, but she held back the words, hid the pain behind one of the masks she'd learned to put on over the past few years.

'I'm fine...honestly. Sorry if I've been a pain to work with but, as I said, I am rather tired today.' She gave a light laugh, thinking wryly what a good actress she'd become, thanks to Matthew. 'I promise I'll do better next week, OK?'

Denis shrugged, plucking his jacket from the peg behind the door to shrug it on. 'Don't worry. We all have our off days, and you're usually on the ball, so I can't really grumble. Now how about a spot of lunch to cheer you up? We can go to Luigi's.'

'Well, I don't...' She hesitated, something in his face making her retrieve the refusal she'd been about to make. If anyone needed cheering up it was Denis himself. She'd never seen him looking so down in the mouth. 'I'd love to, but I can't stay too long. I've got loads to do.'

'A hectic social life. I envy you, Mags. It's just what I could do with right now.'

Denis smiled wryly as he opened the door for her, but Maggie just nodded, making no attempt to tell him that she could write the details of her 'social life' on the back of a postage stamp! The only thing she had planned for the afternoon was collecting Janey from the child minder and going home to catch up on the washing. However, apart from Marie, she'd told no one about her daughter, preferring to keep work and her private life in two completely separate compartments. It had seemed the safest thing to do at the time to avoid Matthew's finding out, but now all that secrecy seemed laughable.

Pain twisted her heart into a knot, but she fought it down as she led the way down the steep flight of stairs from the tiny studio to the street. The restaurant was only a block away, so they opted to walk, Maggie shivering as the wind sliced through the sweater she was wearing.

'Here, have my jacket. We don't want you catching a chill before next week.' With a show of gallantry Denis draped the heavy leather jacket round her shoulders before huddling deeper into the scruffy, disreputable sweat-shirt he wore with an equally disreputable pair of cord jeans. Nobody even at their kindest moment could ever call him the picture of sartorial elegance, but he was a nice man, genuinely kind and considerate, and Maggie silently prayed that her friend would realise that and not let him slip through her fingers. Easy, uncomplicated men like Denis were as rare as diamonds, and Marie would be a fool to lose him by playing silly games.

The restaurant was crowded, the small tables crammed to overflowing with dishes that sent delicious aromas wafting through the air. Maggie sniffed appreciatively as she stepped through the door, suddenly realising just how hungry she felt. She'd been so sick and shaken that morning that all she'd had was a cup of black coffee before she'd left to take Janey to the sitter.

She turned round to tell Denis what a good idea it had been to come, then felt the words die in her throat when she saw the man sitting at a table by the window. The room seemed to distort, going fuzzy at the edges as she met the anger in that cold blue gaze, then Matthew raised his wine glass in a mocking silent toast and suddenly everything shot back into vivid painful focus.

'Ah, Miss Duncan, Mr Morris, how nice to see you again. Please follow me. I have just one table left, which should be perfect for you both.'

In a daze, she followed Luigi across the room, aware that Matthew was watching them every step of the way. She could feel his gaze boring into her back, and she drew in a shuddering breath as she sat down, deliberately keeping her eyes averted from the table by the window. This was the last place she would ever have expected to find him, so that the shock of seeing him was somehow doubly great. Whenever they had eaten out, he had always chosen where they went, formal, expensive restaurants where he was a known and valued client. The Matthew of three years ago would never have chosen this little, casual trattoria with its warm and friendly atmosphere, and somehow it knocked the mental image she had of him slightly out of sync. And that disturbed her more than she could explain.

'Maggie!'

Denis's voice roused her from her reverie, and she blushed when she looked up and found him watching her with open curiosity.

'Well, somehow I don't think a penny would be quite enough for those thoughts. You were miles away then, love, and nowhere pleasant, from the look of it!'

She forced a smile, glad when Luigi offered the handwritten menus and diverted Denis's attention. She bent over her copy, forcing herself to concentrate on the flowing script, but the words kept dancing up and down before her eyes. Slowly her gaze slid across the room, drawn by a power much stronger than her own, and she felt her heart leap when she met Matthew's eyes. Hurriedly she looked away, barely aware that Luigi was speaking, offering his suggestions for the meal. Why did Matthew have to be here today, of all days? All she needed was a bit of breathing-space to recover from last night and she would be on course again, ready to face him and handle anything he chose to throw at her. Now it would be far more difficult to recover her composure.

'Sounds great to me. How about you, Mags? Shall we make that for two?'

'What? Oh, yes, fine. Thanks.'

She had no idea what she'd ordered but she didn't care. All she wanted was to get the meal over and done with, then get away from there as fast as she could. Even now she could feel Matthew watching her, feel his eyes in a way that made her pulse race

and the blood pound in her veins as though these
past three years had never happened, and it
frightened her.

'Isn't that Geoff Graham over there? Remember
him, Maggie? I did that lay-out for him a couple
of months back and you modelled one of the
evening gowns.'

Denis waved a hand across the room and Maggie
followed his bidding, spotting the man sitting with
a group of people at a table by the far wall.

'You don't mind if I just pop over and have a
word with him, do you, love? But there are a couple
of things I've been meaning to ask him about that
spread, and now seems like the ideal opportunity.'

Without waiting for an answer, Denis got up and
crossed the room, leaving Maggie staring after him
in something akin to desperation. At least while
Denis had been there she'd had some measure of
protection, but now she felt completely alone and
defenceless. Nervously she flicked a glance from
under her lashes towards the window, and jumped
violently when she saw Matthew push back his chair
and stand up. She turned her head away, feeling
her heart pounding in her throat, sending the blood
in dizzying waves to her head. He *wouldn't* come
over and speak to her. He was just getting up to
leave, probably as keen as she was not to have to
be in the same room with one another after last
night. He, above all people, wouldn't risk causing
a scene in a public place!

'Seems we are destined to keep on meeting,
Maggie.'

She shuddered as he spoke, her whole body going
rigid in a terrified spasm so that for a moment she

couldn't speak, couldn't find the strength to turn and tell him to go away. How could he do that so easily, send her mind and senses spinning? She wished she knew, wished she could find some cure for it: wished that once and for all she could make herself immune to Matthew Kane and everything he did or said.

Slowly, deliberately, she turned her head and looked at him, forcing herself to meet his eyes with as much calm as she could muster. Once she would have looked at him, her face open, unguarded; now she could only bear to do so from behind the safety of a mask.

'It does indeed. Actually, I'm surprised to see you here at all.' She glanced round the bright room, barely hearing the noisy chatter, barely seeing the other people, aware only of the man who was standing next to her, so close that she could have reached out and touched him if she'd had a mind to. But three years and so much hurt and pain had destroyed that desire in her forever. 'This doesn't strike me as the sort of place *you* would frequent.'

There was a touch of irony in her cool voice and his eyes glinted, Matthew registering it immediately, as she should have known he would. Words and the power of the human voice were his business. He knew only too well how to inject every emotion possible into a brief statement. It was what had brought him to the very pinnacle of his profession as a barrister, that ability to sway a jury by a few well-chosen, eloquently spoken sentences. She was a fool to try to play him at his own game, and Maggie knew it, but she couldn't stop herself from feeling a certain satisfaction when she saw that she had pricked his composure.

'And what makes you say that?' His voice was level, but underneath she could hear the edge of anger, and some little devil inside her spurred her on.

'Why? Because the Matthew Kane I knew would never have lowered himself to eat in a restaurant where the waiters weren't properly dressed in dinner-jackets and where the service wasn't silver!'

He stiffened at the implied insult in the mocking words, seeming to tower over her in the well-cut charcoal suit which emphasised his height and the solid width of his shoulders. 'Nor would the Maggie I knew have been seen dead in public in an outfit like the one you're wearing now!' He skimmed a contemptuous glance over the battered leather jacket which was still draped around her shoulders. 'Seems as if we both might have changed, doesn't it?'

His words stung and she coloured, smoothing a hand defensively down the cracked leather, wishing she'd dressed in something a bit more impressive than the clinging jeans and sweater, topped off by this jacket. 'It's not mine, actually. Denis lent it to me,' she said quickly in way of explanation, then felt her heart leap in alarm as she saw the way his face tightened immediately.

Reaching out, he swept the jacket from her shoulders and flung it over a nearby chair. Instinctively Maggie tried to stop him, then recoiled when he bent closer to her, his eyes burning into hers so that she felt consumed by the fire in their depths.

'I don't want you wearing his things, Maggie. Understand?'

'I...I...' She swallowed hard, turning her head away to break the spell, feeling the anger surging in her breast the very moment she had done so. '*You* don't want me to, Matthew? You really think you have the right to dictate to me?' She laughed lightly, mockingly, enjoying the way the hot colour rimmed his cheekbones as he heard her disbelief. 'Sorry, Matthew, but you're a few years too late to tell me what I can and can't do! Now, if you don't mind, I would prefer it if you left. I want to enjoy this lunch and there won't be much hope of that if you keep on hanging around.'

'And does David know about this...about him?'

He looked across the room at Denis, who was now chatting animatedly to the group he'd joined, blissfully unaware of what was going on, then looked back at Maggie, his lip curling in contempt. 'Or is this another of your little flings, Maggie? That's more like the truth, isn't it, with your track record? I was surprised that you and David are still together. Three years is a long time for you to be satisfied with the same man, but then again, I suppose, there is the child to consider, and even you wouldn't be selfish enough to split her up from her father at such a tender age. So is this how you get round the boredom factor, by meeting your menfriends at lunchtime and having your discreet little affairs while poor trusting David knows nothing about it? Maybe I should have a word with my brother and warn him what a little slut you are, Maggie. After all, blood is thicker than water, so they say, and I wouldn't like him to fall into the same trap I did, even after what happened.'

How could he say that? How could he even think such things, let alone say them, about her? Even while she was trying to understand, she struggled to her feet, her face ashen, her whole body shaking as though she'd been attacked physically not verbally.

'Damn you, Matthew,' she said hollowly, her voice trembling as she fought back the tears. 'Damn you to hell and back for saying such wicked things!'

He caught her arms, stopping her when she tried to push past him, his fingers biting through the soft thin wool of her sweater until they bruised her flesh. 'Oh, I dare, Maggie. I dare that and a whole lot more, if you want to know.' He laughed softly, bending closer so that his breath touched warmly and moistly against her cheek as she turned her face away. 'I've already been to hell, you see. I went there three years ago when you made me a laughing-stock, and I've not forgotten it. I *won't* forget it until I can exorcise the ghosts of everything that happened from my mind!'

She went still, feeling the cold chill of fear invading her limbs. 'What do you mean? It's over between us, Matthew. We're divorced and that's it ... finished.'

He shook his head, all amusement leaving his face. 'It's not over, but it will be...soon.' He caught her chin, forcing her head round so that he could look straight into her eyes. 'I'm going to have you again, Maggie, in every way the word implies, and then, when you are as crazy for me as I was for you three years ago, I'm going to walk out and leave you with your life in tatters.'

'No!' Her voice was just a faint husky murmur when she wanted to shout the denial aloud and keep on shouting it until it gained power and strength enough to quell the cold fear racing through her body. He was just trying to frighten her, making threats he had no hope of achieving without her agreement, and she would never agree to go back to him. Never!

She pulled her arms free and pushed past him, unaware of Denis's startled murmur as she hurried past him without a word and raced out of the door. It was raining outside, a thin fine drizzle which soaked through the fine wool of her sweater in seconds, though she didn't even notice it as she hurried along the street, trying to put as much distance as she could between her and Matthew, but she couldn't run from the words which echoed round and round in her head. No matter how many times she told herself that it had just been a threat, she knew only too well how Matthew had a habit of getting what he wanted!

CHAPTER THREE

'I CAN'T leave you like this, Maggie. Look, I can cancel the flight and stay until you're feeling better. I'm sure Langton will understand once I explain the circumstances.'

Maggie shook her head, and grimaced as the room started to spin. She closed her eyes for a moment, then opened them again to fix David with a firm look.

'You can't do that. You know very well that this is the opening you've been waiting for. If you don't go then Langton will just find someone else and you'll have missed your chance. I'll be fine, honestly. It's just a cold, that's all, and no one has ever died of a common cold, I'm sure!'

She tried to inject a touch of humour into her croaky voice, but she could tell by David's expression that he wasn't convinced, and she hid a sigh.

David had had a real struggle to rebuild his life after the divorce which had isolated him not only from Matthew but from his family. He had resigned from the huge influential firm of lawyers founded by his father, Marcus Kane, determined that the unsavoury publicity surrounding the case should cause no more harm than it had already. At the time he had confessed to her that he'd been glad in a way that he'd been pushed into making such a decision because he'd long come to realise that the law wasn't for him. However, his new choice of career had been a surprise. He had set himself up in business crafting furniture, beautiful, individual pieces, destined to become collectors' items in years to come. In the past year he had just begun to make a name for himself, and this latest commission, to fly over to Dallas to discuss making several pieces for Clark Langton, millionaire owner of Langton Chemicals Inc, could only do him good. It was the real opening he needed, and Maggie knew that there was no way she was going to let him miss out because of her.

Determinedly she stood up, clutching hold of the back of the chair as her rubbery legs threatened to give way. She'd come down with a cold a couple of days previously, but it had seemed impossible to shake it off as she usually did. Instead of feeling better today she felt worse, and secretly she wondered if it was a touch of flu rather than the common cold she'd claimed it to be. Still, at least Janey had shown no signs of catching it yet: she'd been twice as lively as usual, probably missing the company of the other children cared for by the child minder. Maggie hadn't felt well enough to bother struggling out each day to take her to the sitter, nor had she had the need. No one wanted to photograph a model with a pasty face and nose as red as Rudolph's!

'Look, David, you're going to miss your flight if you don't get off. Just make sure you send me a postcard from lovely hot Dallas, eh?'

David sighed, standing up as he lifted his jacket from the back of the chair and slid it on. 'I still don't like the thought of you being here all by

yourself, Maggie. What if you need something?'
He glanced out of the window, his eyes narrowing
on the leaden sky. 'You can't go out in this weather
or you'll be down with pneumonia, not just a cold,
so what do you intend to do about shopping?'

'I'll ring Marie and ask her to pick me up anything I need. The cold will be gone in a day or so.
Stop fussing, David. You're like a mother hen when
you get started!'

David laughed, reaching out to sweep her into
his arms and hug her hard. 'You *need* fussing over,
Miss Duncan. You are the most independent
woman I know and, given an inch, I would fuss
over you a whole lot more!'

There was a strange note in his voice which
Maggie hadn't ever heard before, and she stiffened, reacting instinctively to it. Despite Matthew's
bitter accusations, she and David had only ever been
friends, nothing more, nothing less, but somehow
that note in his deep voice had held more than mere
friendship. She drew back, a tiny frown wrinkling
her brow as she studied his handsome face, but she
could see nothing there to alarm her and she relaxed against him again, feeling the nervous
pounding of her heart subside. She valued David's
friendship so much, knew that it had been the only
thing that had kept her going through all the dark
times. She would hate to lose it, but she would never
risk hurting him by letting him think there could
ever be anything more between them than that. She
had tried and tasted love, savoured the beauty and
magic of it, and suffered the anguish and the pain,
and she would never let herself try it again. In a
way, Matthew had won, she supposed: he had been

the first man she had ever loved, and he would be the last, because she would never risk her heart again.

'It's not just the cold I'm worried about, Maggie, if I'm really honest.' David set her from him, holding her shoulders as he stared into her face. 'I know you don't want to talk about it, but you can't keep burying your head in the sand and pretending it never happened. What if Matthew suddenly decides to come here again?'

Maggie looked away, dropping her eyes to the smooth silk of his grey tie, terrified that he would see the fear his words evoked and wonder about it. It had been a week since she'd seen Matthew in that restaurant, yet she could still feel the terror just as sharply when she remembered what he'd said. She hadn't told David about it, of course. She knew him too well. He would have insisted on going to confront his brother immediately, and that was something she hadn't wanted to happen, partly because she'd been afraid that it would promote the situation, and partly because she still felt guilty that she had been the cause of the rift between them.

Abandoned as a baby, Maggie had been brought up in a series of children's homes and had never known the closeness of family life or enjoyed the bond which could exist between brothers and sisters. At one time she would have done anything in her power to heal the bitter rift between Matthew and David, but there had been little she could do in the face of Matthew's conviction that his suspicions were correct. He had seen the friendship she and David had enjoyed right from the beginning with eyes tainted with jealousy, and that still coloured his judgement today.

She drew in a shaky breath, striving to sound far more confident than she felt. 'He won't come here again. Remember his face that night when he saw you holding Janey? He's convinced she is our child, and that will keep him away from here.' It was what she'd clung to all week, this one hope, and she repeated it now like a charm to ward off another visit from Matthew.

'He's a fool. Anyone can see that she's his daughter!'

'Matthew can't.' She moved away, picking up a rug from the chair and folding it with hands that trembled slightly. 'And it's better that he can't see. I don't want him coming back into my life!'

'Are you sure? Sure that you...well, that you don't want to tell him the truth?' David held his hand up, smiling wryly as she rounded on him, her green eyes flashing. 'OK, OK, sorry I said anything, but I can't help remembering how *you* looked that night, Maggie, as though he had hit you a mortal blow when he failed to recognise Janey as his daughter. I know he hurt you, said and did the most cruel things, but are you absolutely certain that you don't want him to know about her?' He shrugged, his eyes darkening. 'I know I'd hate to be the one not to know if I had a child.'

'Matthew gave up any rights he had to know about Janey when he divorced me. Surely you haven't forgotten what he said, what he accused you and me of doing?' She tossed the blanket aside, her hands clenching into fists at her sides, her face etched with pain-filled memory. 'I haven't forgotten a word, David, not one single word. How could I, when every one is engraved on my heart as a warning?' She drew in a sharp breath, then let it out, forcing herself to relax, terrified that she would say something she shouldn't and alert David to the fact that she had seen Matthew again since that night. David was stubborn in his own way. He would refuse to catch the plane if he had an inkling of what had gone on and what Matthew had threatened. 'Now come along. Out you go, before you miss that flight.'

She shooed him towards the front door, giving him a quick hug when he bent and kissed her cheek, then stood and watched him walk down the path and climb into his car. He started the engine and waved, then drove off, but it was several minutes before Maggie went inside and closed the door. It was the first time that she'd been really and truly on her own since the divorce, the first time that she'd had only herself to rely on without David's comforting presence to fall back on, and suddenly she felt so vulnerable.

What *would* she do if Matthew sought her out again, determined to carry out his threat? She had tried so hard to convince herself that she was over him but for the past week she'd known that that was a lie.

She might hate him for what he had done, but deep inside, in that part of her only he had ever touched, she still responded to him. He'd said that he had ghosts to exorcise, and she could believe that because she had her own ghosts, her own memories, her own foolish, stupid desires to turn back the clock.

If he came and found her again then she would have to fight not only him, but herself as well.

With a weary sigh Maggie stooped down and picked up the last toy to toss it into the bright red plastic box. She straightened up, feeling her head swimming with exhaustion. Janey had been on top form all morning long, rushing about from one project to the next, leaving a wake of toys scattered across the sitting-room floor. Usually Maggie made her daughter clear things up after herself, but today it had seemed too much of an effort. It had been far easier to leave everything until after lunch, when Janey had her sleep.

Shooting a last look round the room to check she'd missed nothing, she walked slowly into the kitchen and filled the kettle before ripping open yet another sachet of the lemon-flavoured drink guaranteed to cure her cold, if she was to believe the manufacturer's claims. She poured hot water into the mug, then carried it back to the sitting-room and sat down, wrinkling her nose in distaste as she took a tentative sip. She leant back in the chair, feeling her legs aching and her head throbbing in that dull, heavy way it had been doing all day since she'd got up. It would be so good to go back to bed and pull the covers over her head until she felt better, but with a young child to take care of there was no chance of that!

The doorbell rang and she jumped nervously, setting the cup aside before scrambling to her feet and rushing to the window to ease the lacy curtain back while she peered out. It was something she had started doing this past week, checking first before she answered the door, wary of finding Matthew standing on the step, but even being prepared for it didn't lessen the shock when she saw his tall familiar figure.

She dropped the curtain and stepped back, pressing a hand to her throat to stem the violent racing of her pulse, feeling her whole body trembling. He had told her so clearly what he intended that day in the restaurant, spelled it out for her in vivid words and even more vivid images, and now she was so afraid that she thought she would faint. It was only a steely determination, hard-won over the past few years, which kept her on her feet and held the blackness at bay.

The bell rang again, longer and louder this time, with a touch of impatience to it, and a faint bitter smile twisted her lips. Matthew hated to be kept waiting for anything. He was used to people jumping when he demanded attention, used to his every command being met instantly, and she could well imagine his growing annoyance when she didn't respond. Well, as far as she was concerned, he could stand out there all day long, ringing the bell, because there was no way on God's sweet earth that she was letting him in!

The bell went again, one long hard peal followed by another and another, and Maggie pressed her hands over her ears to block out the sound, then groaned when she heard a familiar wail from upstairs. All the noise had obviously woken Janey from her nap: now she would be cranky and cross all afternoon.

She hurried from the room and ran up the stairs, lifting the child from her cot and drying her tear-streaked cheeks with a gentle hand.

'Shhh, it's all right, poppet. He'll go away soon.'

Nervously she paced the bedroom floor, Janey cradled close against her shoulder, but after ten minutes more of the bell ringing it was obvious that Matthew had no intention of going away, and her nervousness was starting to affect Janey. The child was sobbing now, her small face puckered up in distress, her red cheeks streaked with tears, and it was that more than anything which made Maggie realise she had to do something to stop the racket from downstairs.

Hitching Janey tighter against her, she ran down the stairs and flung the door open, her green eyes like ice as she glared at Matthew.

'What the hell do you think you are doing? You're frightening Janey half to death with that racket.'

He straightened away from the bell push, raising a hand to brush the ruffled dark hair from his forehead, his face set. 'Don't blame me. You should have answered the door instead of ignoring it.'

'Ignore it? No one could ignore a row like that!' She drew in a shuddering breath, feeling her heart hammering so hard in her chest that it felt as though it might explode any second. But she had to be calm, had to face Matthew with nothing more than indifference, rather than this violent anger he always seemed able to unleash. 'What do you want, Matthew? I thought I made it quite plain the other day that you're not welcome here.'

He raised a dark brow, his mouth curling tauntingly as he slid a glance over her white face. 'And I think *I* made it plain what my intentions are.'

'You're mad, do you hear me? Completely out of your skull if you think I'll ever have anything to do with you again! Now go away and leave me alone before I——'

'Before you what? Run and tell my dear brother?' He smiled coldly, his eyes flat, icy. 'You can't do that, can you? Because David is away in America, leaving you here, all by yourself.'

The shock must have shown on her face because the smile deepened, and instinctively she stepped back, suddenly unsure of what he intended. He took advantage of the moment to push the door further open and step inside the hall, closing it firmly behind him, despite her protests.

'What do you think you're doing? Get out of here at once or I'll call the police and have you arrested!'

'Will you really, Maggie? I don't think so. I'm sure you've had enough sordid publicity to last you a lifetime! And now, of course, there's the child to consider, isn't there? It wouldn't make pleasant reading for her in the future.'

'I hate you, Matthew Kane...hate you!'

'No more than I hate you, Maggie.'

'Then why are you doing this? Why won't you just leave things alone? Surely you can't be enjoying this any more than I am?' The words were a cry of anguish, a plea for understanding, but he appeared indifferent to them, his face betraying nothing but a cold detachment which chilled her to the bone. When he spoke his voice was clear, holding a conviction that made the fear run in ripples down her spine.

'I am not enjoying it, but it is something I have to do for my own peace of mind.' He moved closer, staring straight into her eyes, and she felt the cold blue stare like something physical. 'I've tried to put you out of my mind, tried my damnedest to start afresh, but you're always there, Maggie, always in the back of my mind, a lingering presence, a wound that won't heal until it's lanced.' He reached out and grasped her shoulders, holding her when she would have struggled to free herself. 'The only way I shall ever be free of the past is to go back in time and relive it, drive out the ghosts that haunt me!'

'No!' She shook her head, straining against his hold, hampered by the weight of Janey still held tightly in her arms. 'It *is* over! It was over three years ago: you can't go back, can't change things now!'

His fingers bit into her flesh, hurting her, yet she knew that he was unaware of it. 'It will never be over until I can wipe what you did from my mind. And the only way I can do that is by making you suffer as I suffered!'

She couldn't speak, couldn't move, couldn't find the strength to do anything but stand there, held by his anger, his bitterness, by her own sense of failure. She had given everything to their marriage, but in the end it hadn't been enough.

But she couldn't let him do this now, wouldn't let him destroy both their lives by this insane desire for revenge.

'No, Matthew! You're wrong. You won't achieve anything at all by hurting me. You have to accept what's happened and let it all go, get on with your life as I am trying to get on with mine. Making me suffer won't heal the wound but open it again! Revenge isn't the answer.'

'No?' His voice softened, his eyes holding hers in a way that made the blood rise in her veins, but for the life of her Maggie couldn't tell if it was from fear, or from another reason, far more dangerous to her peace of mind. 'Maybe it isn't the answer, Maggie, but I'll take a chance on being proved wrong. You can deny it all you like, but you still feel something for me the same as I still feel something for you, and until we work that out of our systems then we shall neither one of us be completely free!'

'No!' She spun away from him, clutching Janey so tightly that the child whimpered and started to squirm to be put down. Maggie set her down on her feet and watched her run into the sitting-room, before turning back to Matthew, her face pale and etched with grief.

'You say I still feel something for you; well, you're right, I do, but it isn't love! You can get that right out of your head once and for all!'

'I never said it was.' He laughed softly, his intentions written all over his face as he caught her arms and bent his dark head to brush her mouth with his. Maggie went rigid, her whole body clenching in shock at the soft familiar touch of his lips. She closed her eyes, fighting against the stir of memories, the sudden flare of remembered desire. Matthew had always had this effect on her. He had only to touch her to send her up in flames, wanting nothing more than to feel his hands on her skin, and even now she wasn't proof against him.

Slowly, delicately, his tongue traced round the contours of her lips, teasing, tormenting, awakening those same fires inside her so easily that she could have wept in shame. Was she really so spineless that she would stand here and let him do this to her again? Was she so weak that she would let physical desire cloud her judgement?

She pushed against him, desperate to make him stop, her hands sliding inside the open front of his jacket on to the warm, hair-roughened muscles of his chest under the fine silk of his white shirt, and her mind went spinning out of control, sucked into the maelstrom of the past. Her mouth opened on a helpless moan and he took advantage of it immediately to deepen the kiss, his tongue sweeping erotically round the soft contours of her mouth until she was burning with desire. When his hand slid under the loose hem of her sweater and cupped her breast she arched towards him, aching to feel the touch of his fingers against her nipple, to feel again the magic only he could make.

'Mummy...Mummy, look!'

The childish voice cut through the flames of desire, bringing her back to reality with a speed that left her shocked. Abruptly she pulled herself from Matthew's arms and turned away, pushing the wisps of red hair back from her pale face with hands that trembled. Her whole body was on fire, the blood licking along her veins like flames, her heart beating with a speed and heaviness that made her feel breathless, and a deep pain filled her at her own stupidity.

'Look, Mummy.'

Janey stood in the doorway to the sitting-room, holding a brightly coloured tower of Lego bricks out for her inspection. Maggie forced herself to smile through lips which had suddenly grown stiff. 'That's lovely, darling. Why don't you go and see how big you can make it?'

Janey stared solemnly at her for a moment, then smiled and turned back into the room, humming tunelessly under her breath, obviously unaware of the tension in the hall. How Maggie envied her: how she wished that she could just turn her back on what had happened in the past few minutes, but she couldn't. Matthew would never let her do that, but there was no way she was going to let him take advantage of her weakness either.

She stood up straighter, drawing dignity round her like a cloak as she looked at him. He was standing completely still, a strange expression of deep sadness on his face, which surprised her, but then he caught her glance and his expression altered to one of such satisfaction that she felt herself go cold in fear. He had felt her reaction to him, felt the desire awakening in her body at his touch, but somehow she had to convince him that it meant nothing; that, no matter what, he would never make her fall in love with him again!

'So now you have your proof that I do feel something, Matthew. I don't deny it. You have always been able to make me desire you, but that's all it is and I'm not stupid enough to let you take advantage of the fact!'

He laughed harshly, pushing his hands deep into the pockets of his trousers as he leant almost indolently against the wall while he studied her flushed face. 'Do you really think it's that easy, Maggie? Do you think you can just turn your feelings on and off at will?'

'Of course I can!'

He shook his head, his dark hair catching the light so that it shone with a blue fire. 'No, Maggie. When you lie in bed tonight your body will ache for my touch, your blood stir, waiting for the fire only I can ignite. I know. I've lived with this desire for three years, like a disease, and I've still not found the cure. But I will!'

'No! I won't have anything to do with you, do you hear me? Nothing! Do you really think I'd be fool enough to start all over again?' She laughed bitterly, unaware of the tears which had started to slide down her cheeks. 'I might ache, Matthew, but you'll never know about it because I won't let you ruin my life again as you did before with your insane jealousy.'

'You're just getting hysterical.'

'Am I, indeed? Why, silly me, getting hysterical because my ex-husband has just threatened to tear my life apart!' She drew in a shuddering breath, fighting to stay calm. She had to convince him here and now that he was wrong to attempt such a thing. 'Three years haven't dimmed the memories of what happened, Matthew. I still remember everything you said, how you acted. You blamed David, but he was just the whipping-boy because you were so eaten up with jealousy that every man I came into contact with was, in your eyes, guilty! How many men did you think I'd had affairs with? Two, three . . . three dozen? Come on, Matthew, put a figure on it!'

His face darkened with anger as she taunted him, and he came away from the wall in a rush, but Maggie stood her ground. Suddenly she was tired, tired of being called names, of being blamed for things she had never done and never thought of doing.

'I never even looked at another man when we were married, Matthew. Never even thought about anyone else. You were my whole world and I would have walked barefoot through fire if you'd asked me, but that wasn't enough, was it? You wanted to own me, body and soul, keep me locked away from the world, your own private possession. That was the reason why you made me give up modelling, why you slowly but insistently broke up all the friendships I'd ever made. You isolated me from everyone, and when I, quite innocently, found friendship with your own brother you cast your own interpretation on it. Well, now you've succeeded beyond your wildest dreams because I don't need anyone at all in my life, and especially not you!' She walked to the door and flung it open. 'Now get out of here and don't come back!'

For a moment she thought he was going to ignore her, then slowly he walked towards the door and she let out a sigh of relief, but it was just a shade premature, it seemed. He stopped when he drew level with her, his eyes like ice as he stared down into her face.

'You were so in love with me that you never looked at another man? Is that right?' He caught her chin and lifted her face up when she tried to turn away. 'Well, if that was so then explain how that child comes to be here.' He smiled tauntingly. 'It didn't take you long to get pregnant, did it, especially when you claim that your friendship with David was pure and innocent?' His lip curled in derision. 'That is assuming, of course, that my dear brother is the father, and I expect that is debatable!' He let her go, stepping back a pace, his eyes riveted to the stark pallor of her face. 'You tell a moving tale, Magdalena, but you forget that I know you and what you are capable of. So save all the sob-stories, because they won't work. My mind is still made up and nothing you can say or do will change it!'

'Get out!' It took everything she had, every scrap of strength to force the words out from between her cold lips, but she did, clutching hold of the door, terrified that she would crumple in a heap at his feet.

'Oh, I'm going, but I'll be back, never fear. I'm even more determined than ever to carry out my plan now.'

'Why?' Her voice was a husky murmur, but he heard it and smiled thinly, his eyes glacial as he reached out and ran a finger down her cheek and across the soft, warm swell of her lips.

'For all the reasons I've already told you, plus one more, which even surprises me.'

'What reason?' She jerked her head away from the light touch, feeling the lingering imprint of his flesh on hers like something tangible.

'The child.' He looked past her, and something in his expression made her heart twist in pain. She glanced over her shoulder, fear running through her when she saw Janey standing in the hall watching them. Instinctively she turned to get her, then stopped when Matthew continued, his voice flat and devoid of feeling, yet affecting her far more than any show of anger could have done.

'She could have been our child, Maggie, yours and mine, and I don't think I shall ever forgive you for that!'

Her breath caught and she swung round just in time to see the expression of anguish on his face before he turned and strode away down the path. Slowly she closed the door, lifting Janey into her arms when she ran to her, holding her warm little body close, but even that couldn't dispel the coldness growing in her heart. That Matthew might have wanted a child was something that had never occurred to her, and now it shook her to the very depths. He had hurt her so much, done her an injustice, but had she not served him an even greater one by denying him his child?

CHAPTER FOUR

'COME on, Janey, be a good girl and let Mummy fasten the straps, then we can go home and play.' Maggie forced herself to stay calm as she made yet another attempt to fasten the safety harness in the buggy around Janey's squirming little body, but to no avail. The child wriggled round, pulling herself free as she tried to climb out again.

'No! Naughty girl. Now sit still!' There was an unusually sharp note in her voice, and Janey stared at her in surprise before her face puckered up and she started to cry. Maggie steeled her heart against the pathetic little sound and snapped the belt into place, a faint colour touching her cheeks when she caught the disapproving stare from the elderly woman standing next to her in the shop doorway.

Well, she certainly wasn't going to win any prizes for the perfect mother with this performance, but she didn't feel perfect! She felt dreadful, her head throbbing from lying awake all night, going over everything that Matthew had said, her body racked with shivers from the cold which seemed to be getting worse. It was only the fact that the cupboards were almost bare, and that she couldn't seem to be able to get hold of Marie, that had sent her out to the shops this morning.

Picking up the loaded bags, she set off, her head bowed against the stinging force of the rain that had started to fall. She paused at a side-road to let a car turn, grimacing when it sent a shower of water up her legs. Mopping at her wet jeans, she heaved the pram down off the kerb, then murmured in dismay as one of the front wheels sheared off and rolled away.

Easing the listing pram the rest of the way on to the pavement, Maggie stooped down to pick up the wheel, but one glance was enough to tell her that she wouldn't be able to fix it back into place. The whole fitment had snapped off and it would need welding back.

'Out . . . out . . . out . . . out!'

Janey started to wriggle as she chanted, pulling at the harness to get free, and Maggie made a quick grab for the pram to stop it from tipping over. Quickly she set the bags down and unfastened the straps, catching Janey firmly by the hand when she attempted to run off.

'No!' she said sternly, fixing the little girl with a firm look. 'You must hold my hand, Janey.'

Janey returned the look solemnly, her blue eyes, fringed with the dark lashes that were so like Matthew's, still swimming with tears. Maggie drew in a shuddering breath and straightened abruptly, feeling the pain surge inside her chest.

Was this going to happen every time she looked at Janey now? Was she going to look at the child and think of Matthew? She hoped not. The memories were hard enough to bear without that as well.

'Go . . . go, Mummy.'

Janey tugged on her hand and Maggie forced her mind back to her present predicament. Although she hated to take a chance of the pram's being stolen, she couldn't manage to drag it along with her as well as the shopping and Janey. She would have to leave it here, tucked against the wall, and come back for it later in the car.

It was slow progress carrying the shopping and matching her stride to the little girl's, but Maggie plodded doggedly on, concentrating on getting back home rather than on how rotten she felt, so that when a car drew to a sudden halt alongside her she barely spared it a glance.

'Maggie!'

The sound of her name brought her head round, and she stared at the man sitting in the driver's seat, then felt the blood rush to her head when she met the familiar blue eyes. Just for a moment she faltered, then walked on, stepping up her pace until she was almost dragging Janey along with her. What was Matthew doing here, following her? She had no real idea and no desire to find out. The only way she ever wanted to face him again was on the opposite side of a firmly locked door!

'For heaven's sake! What's got into you, woman? Stop!' He pulled the car alongside her again, winding the window right down as he glared at her, but Maggie ignored him, bending down to scoop Janey into her arms as she hurried along the street. He cursed roughly, slewing the powerful car to a halt a few yards ahead of her before climbing out and barring her path.

'Get out of my way, Matthew,' she ordered, trying to step around him, but he reached out and caught her arm, his long fingers locking painfully around her flesh.

'What is it with you, Maggie?' he ground out, his face set into lines of anger which sent a deep shiver running through her. 'What exactly do you think I'm going to do to you, here in the street?' He glanced round, his mouth curling in derision. 'I'm hardly planning on throwing you down on the pavement and raping you, my sweet!'

'I don't give a damn what you are planning to do!' she shot back, wrenching her arm free. 'I'm not interested in anything you do. I don't want to see you, speak to you, and I most definitely don't want you to touch me! So keep your hands off me, Matthew!'

'Since when? Since when has my touch become so repulsive to you?' His expression altered, his eyes gleaming with tiny blue flames in their depths as they ran over her, down from the wet dark-red strands of hair clinging to her skull to the long slim legs encased in the damp jeans, and smiled mockingly. 'Why lie, Maggie? You admitted yesterday that you aren't . . . how shall I put it? . . . immune to me, so why try to pretend otherwise now, when we both know it's not true?' He moved closer, bending his head to stare straight into her eyes, so that she felt a ripple of deep shock course through her, as though he had actually touched her. 'That was the one thing we never had any problems with when we were together, Maggie. Even towards the end of our marriage, we still felt this same desire for one another's body.'

She couldn't seem to breathe, couldn't seem to drag her eyes from his as the memories came back of how it had been for them together, and her face flushed.

'You remember, don't you, Maggie, how it was? Your skin touching mine, your heart beating in the same rhythm as my heart, our bodies moving together, becoming one?' His voice was so soft, so deliciously, enticingly soft, that she almost moaned aloud at the torment he was inflicting. She didn't want to remember this, didn't want to feel again the sensations he had always been able to make her feel when he had held her in his arms and made love to her.

'Stop it, Matthew,' she said harshly. 'I don't know what kind of a game you think you're playing now, but stop saying such crazy things!'

'Crazy? No, they're not crazy. It's the truth, and you know it is; that's why you're so afraid. But you can't keep on hiding from the truth, dearest Maggie. You, above all people, should know that it has a nasty habit of surfacing, and, frankly, I have no intention of letting you hide from it any longer!' His face hardened as he reached out and ran a finger slowly down the wet curve of her cheek before letting it come to rest on the tiny pulse which was beating wildly at the base of her neck. 'Feel it, Maggie? Feel how your body responds to me, even though you don't want it to?' He laughed, suddenly, harshly, and she shrank back so that his hand slid away from her throat. 'It's gratifying to learn just how responsive you still are, my sweet. It will make my task that much easier for me!'

'You're mad, completely insane, if you think I'll let you get close enough to do that to me again!' She tossed the wet hair from her eyes, feeling the fear curling along her veins, ripple after ripple of it.

'We shall see, I expect, but surely you haven't forgotten how determined I can be when I want something, Maggie? And how I do tend to get my own way most of the time? Still, perhaps this isn't the time or the place to continue the discussion. Come along.'

He caught her arm again to lead her along the pavement, but Maggie resisted, her eyes huge in the ashen oval of her face.

'Stop that! What are you trying to do? Where are you taking me?'

He sliced her a sardonic glance, running a hand over his wet hair before looking up at the sky. 'Home, out of this rain, of course.'

'I don't need you to take me home. I can get there by myself, thank you very much!'

'I don't doubt you can. One thing you were always capable of was taking care of yourself! However, it would be a less than gentlemanly thing to do to get in the car and drive off, leaving you here in the rain like this.'

'You were never a *gentleman* in my eyes, Matthew! So don't worry about ruining your image.'

There was a cutting note in her voice but he ignored it, his face quite dispassionate as he stared calmly back at her. 'Then maybe it's about time I tried to improve my image, isn't it? But if you won't accept for your own sake then think about the child, Maggie. She looks half frozen to me.'

It was the way he said it, his deep voice both flat and devoid of emotion as he drew her attention to Janey, that sent a sudden and quite unexpected shaft of pain into Maggie's heart. It was quite ridiculous to feel affected by it, yet for some reason she could feel tears stinging her eyes.

'Her name is Janey,' she said woodenly. 'Is it so difficult to remember that?'

He shrugged, glancing dismissively at the small figure she held in her arms. 'Not if it means that you will stop this silly arguing and get into the car. I'm sure that *Janey* will be far happier out of this downpour.'

Hearing her name, Janey swung round to stare solemnly at the tall man standing in front of her, before her face broke into a sudden smile. With lightning speed she lurched towards him, leaning dangerously from Maggie's hold to wrap her arms around Matthew's neck and cling on like a monkey.

'Stop that, Janey!'

Hurriedly Maggie tried to break the child's hold, but she hung on grimly, tilted at an awkward angle until Matthew had little choice but to lift her into his arms completely.

Janey laughed, her small face flushed with pleasure as she studied his face before reaching out to run a plump little hand across his chin where the shadow of beard darkened his skin.

'Prickles,' she said clearly, looking to Maggie for confirmation.

Maggie flushed, avoiding Matthew's eyes as she nodded. Janey had always been fascinated by the roughness of David's chin when he had visited them without bothering to shave first, but it surprised her that she should afford Matthew the same interest.

'Strange, but she doesn't look a bit like my dear brother, does she, Maggie? Hasn't that made him...well, faintly concerned about her parentage?'

There was a cold note of speculation in Matthew's voice, and Maggie felt the embarrassment fade under the force of a sharp fear. What did he mean by that? Surely he wasn't already suspicious, suddenly recognising how like himself Janey was?

'David isn't like that,' she said quickly. 'He wouldn't need proof!'

'Then he must be a lot more trusting than I ever was.' He laughed shortly, his eyes skimming over the child's face again. 'Knowing you as I do, Maggie, I would have needed blood tests if you had ever come to me and claimed that a child you were carrying was mine!'

It was what she had always known right from the beginning, so it shouldn't have hurt so much to hear him state it so coldly, but it did. She reached over and snatched Janey from his arms, pain darkening her eyes. 'David isn't like you, Matthew. Thank goodness!'

His face hardened, his eyes icy as they met hers. 'I don't doubt that for a moment, but he'll learn! One day he'll wake up and realise what you're really like. You're very good at projecting that sweetly innocent image, but we both know what you're really like, don't we?' He caught her by the shoulders and held her when she started to turn away. 'He might start learning that lesson sooner than you imagine if you aren't more careful. There could have been other people at that restaurant the other day who saw you with your ''friend''. All it would take is a chance word, and then perhaps David will realise what a blind fool he's been to be taken in by that sweet little façade!'

'Why, Matthew? Why are you doing this? How can you say such terrible things?' she whispered brokenly.

He let her go, his face a blank mask. 'You know why. I explained it all to you.'

'I won't let you do it! I won't let you destroy my life again the way you did before!' She was trembling all over but she made herself stand and face him, held not by courage but a fear of what he would do if she didn't manage to convince him how wrong it was. Rain was beating down now, soaking into her coat and into the pale soft fabric of Matthew's light grey suit, but she was as unaware of it as she was unaware of the glances from passers-by who seemed to sense the tension.

Three years ago she had stayed silent, overcome by the agony of hearing his bitter accusations, but now there was Janey to consider. If he hurt her then he would hurt Janey, and she would never allow that to happen while she had breath in her body enough to fight him.

'I am asking you one last time to stop this, Matthew, before more people get hurt.'

He raised a dark brow, his chiselled mouth curving upwards in derision. 'And if I don't?'

'Then I shall obtain a court order to keep you away from me!'

'Oh, so little Maggie has started to grow up, has she? Started using adult threats?' He laughed softly as he moved closer to her, his eyes glittering with amusement. 'Get your court order if it will make you feel better, but it won't stop me.'

'Of course it will! Do you really think that you can ignore a thing like that? No one is above the law, not even you, the great Matthew Kane!'

He caught her chin, his fingers sliding across her damp skin in a light caress that made her burn as he lifted her face to stare deep into her eyes, and Maggie trembled at the expression on his face.

'By the time I have finished, Magdalena, you won't want any court orders to keep me away. You will be so desperate for me again that that will be the last thing on your mind! I can guarantee it!' He let her go, studying her shocked face in silence for a moment. 'Now are you going to accept my offer of a lift home or not?'

She shook her head, unable to find her voice to refuse, feeling her heart pounding sickeningly in her chest.

'Fair enough; if that's your decision I won't bother arguing with you any more. You can have your own way for once, but enjoy it, my sweet. There won't be many more such occasions when you'll call the shots!'

He turned away, striding towards the car to climb inside and start the engine, leaving Maggie staring after him. She wanted to call him back, to make him...beg him to stop this cruel game, but the words seemed to be lodged in her throat.

Holding Janey tightly in her arms, she watched as he drove away with a swish of tyres, hearing what he had said echoing round and round inside her head. She should have felt shocked, angry, afraid...any emotion more suited to such threats. So why did she suddenly, shockingly, feel the first stirrings of a heady excitement? And why should

she feel as though she had just woken from a deep
sleep and was once more alive? Surely Matthew
wasn't drawing her under his spell again so soon?

The thought stayed with her for the rest of the day,
leaving her drawn and tense by the time evening
fell. She gave Janey her supper, then got her bathed
and ready for bed, thankful that the child was so
worn out from the walk back from the shops that
she fell asleep almost at once.

Leaving the bedroom door open just a crack, she
went back downstairs, feeling shivers racing through
her, despite the fact that she seemed to be running
a temperature. The soaking she'd got walking back
from the shops had done nothing for the cold, and
if she was sensible she would get herself something
to eat and then go to bed and try to get some sleep.
It was only the thought of spending another night
lying awake thinking about Matthew that stopped
her.

She went into the kitchen and opened the fridge
to examine its contents, but there was nothing to
tempt her. She didn't feel like eating, just as she
hadn't felt like it all day since that confrontation,
and she hated herself for her own weakness. How
could she be so foolish as to let Matthew affect her
like this again after all that had happened between
them?

Closing the fridge door, she wandered into the
sitting-room and switched on the television, forcing
herself to concentrate on the thrice-weekly soap
opera that was being screened, desperate to keep
her mind busy. When the doorbell suddenly rang
she jumped, her face paling in sudden fear. She ran

to the window and pushed the curtain aside, terrified whom she might see standing outside, then felt her legs go weak with relief when she recognised Marie.

She hurried along the hall and opened the door, shivering violently as a blast of wintry air hit her. 'Come in. Am I glad to see you? Where have you been? I tried to get you earlier today, but there was no answer when I phoned the flat.'

Marie stepped into the hall, unbuttoning the elegant leather coat she was wearing before running a hand over her windblown black hair. She was an exotic-looking woman, her olive skin, black hair and eyes betraying her Latin ancestry. She always managed to look both elegant and sultrily glamorous, as she did tonight, but there was an aura of tension about her which surprised Maggie.

'I hope you don't mind me calling like this, Maggie, but I needed someone to talk to.'

'Of course I don't! Come into the sitting-room and tell me what's wrong, but don't get too close to me. I rather think this cold is trying to turn itself into flu, and Denis will be livid if you fall sick as well as me!'

'I very much doubt that! Denis wouldn't miss me if I dropped down dead at his feet, from what I can tell.'

Maggie shot her a swift look but said nothing until they had sat down. 'Have you and Denis had an argument or something?'

Marie shook her head, crossing her long slim legs as she reached for a cigarette from her bag and lit it with hands that trembled slightly. 'No. How can you argue with someone who is practically unaware of your existence?'

'That's not true. Denis is more than just aware of you!'

'Is he?' Marie gave a tremulous smile, her huge eyes brimming with tears. 'That wasn't the impression I got today at the studio. He barely managed to spare me a word apart from a few curt instructions. Why, a dummy would have received more attention than he gave me!'

'Maybe Denis isn't too certain that you *want* any of his attention.' Maggie leaned forward, handing her friend a tissue from the box on the table. 'Look, Marie, tell me to mind my own business if you want, but how do you really feel about Denis? Are you in love with him?'

Marie flushed, looking down at the glowing tip of her cigarette before she ground it out in the ashtray with a grimace. 'It's that obvious, is it?'

'No, it isn't. In fact, it's only recently that I've been putting two and two together and starting to get the picture.' Maggie smiled. 'You and Denis are a pair, you know. There he is, eating his heart out for you, thinking that you don't give a damn about him, while you are going through exactly the same about him!'

'Eating his hear . . .' Marie shook her head, her eyes glittering with a wild surge of excitement she couldn't quite hide. 'No, you're wrong. He doesn't give a toss about me. He made it only too plain today.'

'Did he? Or was it more a case of his caring too much, and being afraid of you rejecting him? Think about it, Marie. Have you ever given him an inkling of how you feel? Maybe if you did you would be...well, surprised, to say the least.'

'Do you think so? Oh, Maggie, I just don't know what to do. I've never felt like this before, all sort of mixed up and unsure. One minute I think to myself that it's all imagination, that I *don't* give a damn about him, and the next...' She shrugged expressively, leaning forward to look imploringly at Maggie. 'Tell me what I should do, Maggie.'

'Phone Denis...now. It's not late, and surely you can think up some sort of a pretext? But if you love him, Marie, then don't just let him slip through your fingers. He's a good man, a nice man, and you would be a fool to let him go if you really care about him.'

It was so easy to give advice, to see another's problems and the solutions to them, yet so difficult to solve one's own, and the bitter irony of the situation struck Maggie sharply. If only she could tell Marie about her problem and have her offer a solution, but she couldn't. Although her friend knew all about Janey's existence, she knew nothing about Matthew's being her father. Maggie had guarded that secret, trusting it to no one apart from David, terrified that it could come out one day if too many people knew.

'I...I think I will. Do you mind if I use your phone, Maggie, and do it now, before my courage deserts me?'

'Be my guest. Look, I'll just go and pour us both a drink while you make that call. I'm sure we could both do with one. I'm afraid there's not much choice, just sherry or a drop of brandy left from last Christmas. Which will you have?'

'Better make mine a brandy. I might need the booster if this call goes wrong!'

'It won't.'

Leaving her friend to make the phone call, Maggie went through to the dining-room, where she kept the few bottles of spirits she had in the sideboard. She took her time pouring the drinks, giving Marie a chance to talk to Denis without any interruptions. It was only when she heard the tinkling sound of the receiver's being replaced that she picked up the glasses and went back into the other room.

'Well? How did it go?'

Marie's face was glowing with soft colour, all traces of tears disappeared. 'He invited me round for a drink.'

'Did he indeed? Well, you're not going to need this, then, are you?' She put the brandy glass down on the side-table, smiling at the dazed expression of happiness on Marie's beautiful face. They had been friends for several years now but it was the first time that she had ever seen the other woman looking so flustered and unsure of herself. It reminded her so sharply of how she had been when she'd met Matthew and suddenly realised that she was falling in love with him. It had been the most wonderful time of her life, those first few months, consumed by the love she had felt for him. It had only been later that the problems had begun.

'Are you sure you're feeling all right, Maggie? Here I am rambling on about my problems, without a thought to how you're feeling.'

Marie was studying her with concern, and hastily Maggie dragged her thoughts back to the present, aware that these flashes back to the past were happening far too often recently thanks to Matthew coming so unexpectedly back into her life. 'I'm fine, really. I just seem to be running a bit of a temperature tonight, that's all. But don't worry about me. Did you come in your car tonight?'

Marie shook her head. 'No, I felt like a walk, to clear my head, so I left it behind.'

'Then I'd better ring for a taxi for you. Denis's flat is way across town.'

'Would you? And if you don't mind I'll just pop upstairs and touch up my face while we're waiting for it to get here. I may as well go to meet that man with all the flags flying!'

Maggie laughed, picking up the phone to make the call as Marie hurried from the room. Denis wasn't going to know what had hit him tonight!

Marie was still upstairs when a car drew up outside. Calling a warning to her friend, Maggie hurried along the hall to answer the door to the taxi driver's knock, then felt her head swim with shock when she found Matthew once again on the step.

He smiled faintly, pushing his hands deep into the pockets of the heavy sheepskin jacket he was wearing as he leaned a shoulder indolently against the door-frame. 'You always manage to look so surprised to see me, Maggie, yet I can't imagine why. I've given you fair warning what I intend, so it should come as no surprise to see me here.'

'I...I...' Instinctively she glanced back along the hall, but there was still no sign of Marie. The last thing she wanted was another scene in front of her friend, although she knew that Marie would support her wholeheartedly in any confrontation.

She had always been an intensely private person, and something inside her shrank from drawing an outsider into the bitter arguments which always flared up between her and Matthew. However, it seemed that Matthew interpreted the quite innocent action in a way she had never expected.

He straightened abruptly, his face livid with anger as he pushed her aside and walked into the hall and slammed the door. 'All right, who is he, Maggie?'

'What? Look, Matthew, I don't know what you think——'

He cut her off, such icy fury in his deep voice that she backed away from him, suddenly afraid. 'You can cut out all the bluff, for a start! My goodness, I, above anyone, should know what you're like, but I never really expected this! How long has David been away now...a couple of days? It didn't take you long to get fixed up with someone else, did it, sweetheart? Who is he, Maggie? That guy I saw you with the other lunchtime, or someone fresh to amuse yourself with and pass a few *lonely* hours?'

'How dare you?' She stiffened as the words hit home, her face paling with an anger almost equal to his. 'Get out!'

He shook his head, his face filled with a mocking contempt. 'Before I've had a chance to meet your new "friend"? That wouldn't be polite. After all, I'm sure there are a few things I can tell him about you that he would be most interested to hear. No one knows your likes and dislikes quite the way I do!'

He brushed past her and walked into the sitting-room his eyes sweeping round the cosy room before coming to rest on the two glasses standing on the table. He picked up the brandy, swirling the liquid round and round in the glass, his eyes like chips of ice as they met hers. 'A few drinks . . . to get you both in the right mood, eh? I wonder what David would say about you using his brandy to entertain your gentlemen friends.'

She couldn't take any more, couldn't stand to listen to any more of his comments that made her stomach churn with sickness. Reaching out, she slapped the glass from his hand, her whole body shaking, too incensed to heed the sudden hot glitter in his eyes. 'That's enough! More than enough. Get out!'

She swung round to march towards the door, then gasped with shock when he caught her arm and hauled her back.

'I shall go when I am good and ready to, Maggie. Not a moment before! What are you afraid of? That I shall say something indiscreet and let your "friend" know what kind of a woman you are? In fact, why not let him get a good idea right away? If I'm not mistaken, that's him coming downstairs now.'

'What are——? Ohhh!' The breath left her body as he pulled her to him, holding her so tightly in his arms as he bent and covered her mouth with his that Maggie found it impossible to break free from the cruel kiss. Behind her she heard the sound of a footstep on the polished wooden floor, then a soft gasp of surprise as Marie walked into the room and saw them.

Matthew stiffened, his arms bruising as they contracted around her before abruptly he let her go. Maggie moved away from him, her legs trembling as she rubbed a hand over her mouth to wipe away the burning imprint of his lips, but it lingered.

'I...I'm sorry, Maggie, but I had no idea that...that...' Marie's voice tailed off, her face a study of embarrassment as she looked from Maggie to the tall dark-haired man who was standing there like stone, and Maggie felt the most ridiculous urge to giggle. It wasn't a laughing matter, of course, but there was just something about the situation that struck her as funny. What a come-uppance this must be for Matthew, to find that her friend was another woman!

A chuckle of laughter broke from her lips, followed by another and another until her whole body was shaking helplessly with it.

'Stop that, Maggie!' Matthew caught her by the shoulders and shook her hard, but she couldn't seem to stop, although for some funny reason the laughter seemed to be coming from a distance rather than from her lips. Then suddenly everything started to fade, the room going dark, and with a tiny moan she slid to the floor in a faint.

CHAPTER FIVE

MAGGIE came to slowly, turning her head away from the light cast by the lamp. Just for a moment she couldn't understand what was wrong, why she should feel so strangely disorientated, then suddenly it all came flooding back.

Abruptly she tried to sit up, groaning as the room tilted sickeningly, then fell weakly back against the cushions and closed her eyes again.

'Lie still. You'll only make yourself feel worse by trying to get up too soon.'

The sound of the familiar voice startled her, and she turned her head and opened her eyes again, feeling herself grow cold when she saw Matthew sitting in a chair drawn up next to the sofa. He studied her in silence for a minute, his blue eyes unreadable as they skimmed over her pale face, and Maggie flushed, hating him to see her when she was so vulnerable.

'How do you feel now?'

His tone was distantly polite, far removed from the anger of before, and Maggie strove to match it.

'I'm fine. I must apologise for being such a nuisance. I have never actually fainted before.'

Something flashed in his eyes, an emotion so quickly seen that she barely had time to recognise it before he stood up and walked across to the table to pick up the glass of sherry. Maggie watched him,

73

wondering if she'd been mistaken, because just for
a moment there she'd thought she'd seen regret on
his face, but that couldn't be right. The Matthew
she remembered didn't know the meaning of the
word. He had always been so assured of his actions
that regret was an emotion he'd had little experience of.

He came back and handed her the glass, his hands
impersonal as he helped her to sit up against the
cushions. Maggie sipped the drink, feeling the
coolness sliding down her dry throat and easing
some of the tension from her, but nothing could
ease the nagging ache of that last dreadful scene.
She had known what Matthew thought of her and
how cruel he could be with his unjust accusations,
but nothing could have prepared her for the sheer,
overwhelming force of his anger before. Heaven
knew what might have happened if Marie hadn't...

She gasped, setting the glass down with a clatter
as she looked round the room, but there was no
one else there apart from her and Matthew.

'Your friend left. A taxi arrived for her and I
managed to convince her that you would be quite
safe with me, although she seemed rather reluctant
to take my word on it and leave.'

Maggie shrugged, feigning indifference, wishing
selfishly that Marie had stayed. 'That's all right.
She had to go across town to meet someone. I
wouldn't have expected her to stay when there was
no real need.'

'So she said.'

His voice was bland, so why did she have the
sudden uncomfortable feeling that that hadn't been
the only thing that Marie had said? She shot him

a quick look but there was little on his face that would give her an answer. She could only pray that Marie had been discreet and not told Matthew too much. He had a talent for discovering things, honed to perfection, thanks to his profession, and the thought of his finding out things about her that she didn't want him to know was unsettling. To give Matthew that sort of an advantage was asking for trouble.

Abruptly she swung her legs down off the sofa, holding herself rigid against the wave of dizziness, suddenly anxious to get him out of the house.

'For heaven's sake, Maggie, take it easy!' He bent down, trying to ease her back against the cushions, but she pushed him away.

'I'm all right! Just leave me alone. I'll be fine.'

'Will you, indeed?' He straightened, towering over her as he stood next to the sofa, so close that it was impossible for her to stand up without bumping into him.

'Of course I will!' she snapped, pushing back the tumbling mass of hair which had worked itself loose from the tidy chignon she had secured it into.

'Well, I'm afraid that I beg to differ. You look dreadful, if you'd like to know, and if I'm not mistaken you're running a temperature. It's little wonder that you fainted.' He reached out to press the back of his hand against her forehead to test her temperature, and Maggie flinched, brushing his hand away.

'Stop that! I don't need you to tell me how I feel, Matthew. If I say I will be fine then that's it, end of story! Now I shall be grateful if you would just leave.' She stood up abruptly, forcing him to take a step backwards, then moaned in distress as a wave of nausea hit her. Hand pressed to her mouth, she stumbled from the room and into the kitchen, only just making it to the sink before she threw up.

'Come on, you'll be all right now.' He must have followed her, because when the spasms had finally passed he slid a firm arm around her waist and supported her back into the sitting-room to sit her down once more on the sofa. He left the room, then reappeared a moment later with a cold cloth in his hands and proceeded to wipe it gently over her face and down her neck. Maggie closed her eyes, wishing the ground would open up and swallow her, hating herself for making such a show of herself like that in front of him.

'You need to get to bed. Do you think you can stand up?' His voice was soft, filled with a note that sounded almost like tenderness, and her eyes shot open in surprise. Just for a moment, for one precious second, her eyes met his and suddenly all the anger, all the animosity, faded. Was there just a chance that somehow they could work things out, talk to one another as they hadn't done three years ago?

'Matthew, I...'

He stood up, tossing the cloth on to the table, his face devoid of all expression. 'I think it would be better if you let me help you upstairs.'

Maggie shuddered, dropping her eyes to her hands, clasped in her lap so tightly that the knuckles gleamed bone-white through the delicate pale skin. What a fool she was, what a stupid, mindless fool even to think of such a thing! Matthew didn't want to talk and work things out. He wanted revenge!

In silence she let him help her from the room and up the stairs, too shaken by her stupidity to argue. She didn't want another scene; she just wanted him to go, to leave her house and her life, but she knew it was never going to be that easy.

Thrusting the bedroom door open with his shoulder, he helped her into the room and ran an assessing glance round at the pale peach-tinted walls, the peach and white spread on the bed, the pine furniture. Maggie had decorated the room herself, quite deliberately choosing colours and furniture in direct contrast to that in the bedroom she and Matthew had shared when they had been married. That room had been furnished with antiques, rich fabrics, the very best that money could buy, but she had never felt at ease in that room, never felt that it had been *her* bedroom. It had been Matthew's room, decorated according to his tastes, as had all the rooms in the large elegant house he'd bought for them, overlooking the park.

He had sold the house after the divorce and, although it had surprised her, Maggie had felt no sense of sorrow at the sale. It had never been her home: there had been nothing in it that she had chosen for the elegant rooms. It had all been Matthew's. He had taken over her life from the beginning of their relationship, and that house had been the testimony of it.

Now, as she saw him looking round the fresh, uncluttered room, she was suddenly glad that he would see the differences and realise how determinedly she had tried to put their marriage from her life.

However, he said nothing as he helped her to the bed, and sat her down before standing back and studying her for a moment. 'You look a bit better than you did before downstairs, but you ought to get some rest. Can you manage by yourself, or do you need some help getting undressed?'

'No!' Her heart shook at the thought and she looked away, terrified of what he might see in her face. 'I'll be fine now. I appreciate your help, but there's no need to trouble yourself further on my account.'

He smiled almost gently, but there was nothing gentle about his eyes as they lingered meaningfully on her flushed cheeks. 'I see the idea of having me help you disturbs you, Maggie. We were married, don't forget, and it wouldn't be the first time that I've helped you get undressed!'

A spasm ran through her, a sudden hot flare of longing so intense, so fierce, that it shook her to the depths. It would be so easy to give in to this desire that Matthew had always been able to unleash inside her, but she had to fight it, had to remember what had happened the last time. She had given herself to him then both willingly and joyfully, wanting only to belong to him as she had never belonged to anyone before in her life. She had loved him so much, but even that hadn't been enough to make the relationship work, so how could it work now when all it meant to him was a chance to get even, to salve the bitterness that still filled him?

'I think it would be better if you left now,' she said quietly. 'I don't need any help. I can manage perfectly well by myself, thank you.'

He shrugged lightly. 'As you wish. You seem to have become very independent over the last few years.'

'I've had to. Bringing up a child alone isn't easy.'

One dark brow winged skywards and he smiled tauntingly. 'Hardly alone, surely? What about her father? Surely David has been involved in her up-bringing and will continue to be involved?'

She hated herself for the unconscious slip, silently cursing her wayward tongue and the fact that he could always disturb her so much and make her forget. 'Of course he has. Stop trying to twist everything I say, Matthew. You know very well what I meant!'

'Do I? Frankly, I'm not so sure of that.'

'Stop it! If this is another of your little games then forget it right now. I'm tired and I want to go to bed. What I don't want is yet another pointless discussion going round and round in circles while you try to twist every single thing I say!' She could feel her heart pounding, feel the blood lying thick and heavy along her veins, and she stood up, walking over to the door to hold it so tightly that her fingers started to go numb from the pressure. 'Please leave now. There is nothing more that you and I have to say to one another.'

'What are you so afraid of, Maggie? I thought at first that you were just nervous about meeting me again after the way we parted, but it's more than that, isn't it? You're not just uncomfortable, you're afraid. So what exactly are you trying to keep from me?'

He crossed the room to stand in front of her, so close that she could feel the heat from his lean body, smell the faint familiar aroma of soap and clean skin which was so intrinsically his. She drew back at once, her hand trembling as she clutched hold of the door, feeling the fear filling her, absorbing her, blotting out her ability to think.

'Tell me, Maggie. Tell me.'

His voice was low, deep, persuasive, and she drew in a shuddering breath as she realised what he was doing, how he was trying to manipulate her by assessing her reactions and trying to stampede her into saying something betraying. In the early days of their relationship she had often gone to the courts and watched him using this same lethal skill to cross-examine a witness. At first she had been full of admiration for the way he could elicit information in such a way, but later, when he had turned that talent in her direction, she had grown to hate it.

'You're just being fanciful, Matthew, allowing your imagination to get the better of you. I have nothing to hide.' She smiled, her lips drawn back into a mere travesty of amusement. 'Now, if you have quite finished this ridiculous interrogation then I suggest you leave. I don't think that I am the only one who needs to get some rest tonight!'

'Oh, I'm not so tired, Maggie, that I start imagining things.' He stretched out his hand and ran it down her arm, smiling thinly when she immediately snatched her arm away. 'You're trembling, Maggie, but why? Fever? Desire? Or fear?'

'Neither! None! I... Just leave, Matthew. Now!'

'I'm going, but before I do just answer me one question—to satisfy my curiosity, you understand. Are you and David still living together?'

'You already know the answer to that!' she snapped.

'I thought I did until tonight, until your friend said something that made me start to wonder, and now that I've seen this room I'm convinced that the situation isn't quite what you've led me to believe.'

'My room?' She looked round the bedroom, wondering if she was going crazy, or if, somehow, the desire for revenge had unhinged him in some way.

'Yes, your room.' He laughed softly, something in the deep sound that brought her eyes back to him, and she felt herself grow cold when she saw the calculation on his face.

'It is *your* room, then, Maggie, isn't it?'

'Of course it is! Whose room would you expect it to be?'

'Why, no one's... apart from David's as well! Forgive me if I'm wrong, but doesn't it strike you as odd, seeing as you and David are living here together, that this very feminine room contains only a single bed? It makes me wonder if this relationship with my brother is all it is made out to be. And do you know what interests me most about this fascinating little discovery, Maggie?'

'What?' Her voice was little more than a whisper, but he heard her. Catching hold of her chin, he tilted her face to smile into her shocked eyes.

'The reason why you have been trying to keep up this pretence!'

He let her go, holding her gaze as he bent and brushed her mouth with his in a deliberate caress before walking from the room.

Maggie closed the door, leaning back against its support as her legs started to buckle. She was shaking so violently that she felt like a puppet being jerked about on the end of invisible strings, her limbs out of control, just as her life seemed to be slipping out of control. Somehow she had to stop Matthew from finding out about Janey, but how? How could she fight him when he knew her so well that everything she did was an open book to him?

Not surprisingly, she slept badly, tossing and turning restlessly until dawn broke, when she finally slid into a deep sleep, to awake later with a heavy head and the dry taste of fear in her mouth from the dreams she'd had. She lay quite still for a moment, letting her mind shake off the clinging webs of the dream that had been part nightmare, then glanced at the bedside clock and gasped in alarm when she saw that it was way past ten a.m.

Tossing back the bedclothes, she ran along the landing to Janey's room, wondering why the child hadn't come in and woken her earlier. Janey never slept past seven a.m., her own in-built alarm bringing her awake each morning at that hour, but apparently today had been the exception. She must have been more tired by that walk than Maggie had realised.

She hurried into the room then stopped dead when she saw the empty bed. With a murmur of alarm, she turned and ran down the stairs, quaking at the thought of what an unsupervised two-year-old could get up to, but nothing could have prepared her for what she found in the sitting-room.

Her face went first ashen with shock then was suffused with colour when Matthew looked up at her abrupt entrance, smiling calmly at her from where he lay, sprawled across the floor, working on a complex structure made from Janey's building blocks.

'Just in time. What do you think? Should I opt for a career change and go into architecture, or should I stick to what I know?' He looked back at the oddly shaped construction, his mouth curling attractively as he smiled at the little girl, who was sprawled next to him on the carpet. 'What do you think? Good?'

Janey nodded, her dark curls dancing around her face. 'Good,' she repeated before scrambling up to run to Maggie.

Maggie picked her up and hugged her close while she kissed the smooth little cheek, feeling her throat close with tears. It had been so poignant to see them like that when she'd walked into the room, lying there so close together, one dark head next to the other. It was something she had used to dream of, having Matthew back and watching him playing with his child. Now it filled her with a huge sense of loss to realise that it had just been a fluke to witness it.

Swallowing hard, she set Janey gently back on her feet, smoothing a hand over her tousled hair. 'Go tidy your bricks up now, darling, while I get you some breakfast. You must be hungry.'

Janey shook her head, pointing at Matthew, who was still lying on the floor. 'Matthew made me some.'

'Oh.' Nonplussed, Maggie stared at him, unaware of the softness that lingered on her face, an echo of all those foolish dreams she'd harboured over the years.

'I didn't like the idea of leaving you alone when you weren't well, so I slept down here on the couch until this young lady came down and found me at some unearthly hour. She said that she wanted cereal, so I gave her some. I hope that was all right?'

'Well—er—yes. Thank you. But I never expected that you would stay. You should have told me what you were planning on doing.'

'And had you getting yourself all worked up about it? I don't think so!' He smiled easily, rolling lithely to his feet, obviously unworried by what had happened. How Maggie envied him his self-possession! He was right, of course, she would never have agreed to his staying the night, even if she had been dying. It made her feel . . . strange just to think of it now, as though by the very act of staying the night under her roof he had started to come back into her life.

She searched frantically for something to say to disabuse him of that idea, and he seemed to read her mind in that infuriating way he had.

'No strings attached, Maggie. Last night was a one-off to ease my conscience.'

'I didn't think you had a conscience!' she snapped back, annoyed.

He laughed, ignoring the waspish comment as he began to stretch his cramped muscles, drawing her attention disturbingly to the lean, hard strength of his body. He had always been superbly fit, taking and enjoying regular exercise to combat what could be a sedentary lifestyle, but as she watched him now, clad only in the clinging knit shirt and slim-fitting black trousers, she could see that he had lost weight so that his body was honed to a perfect symmetry of pure muscle without an ounce of superfluous fat.

In a slow sweep her eyes travelled over him, learning the lines of his body again, which she had used to know so well, before coming back to his face, and she felt shock run along her veins when she saw the naked hunger in it. Drawn by an almost irresistible power, she took a slow, dazed step towards him, then stopped abruptly when her bare foot grazed against something hard. She glanced down, staring at the coloured building block, feeling all the madness draining from her as reality came rushing back.

She turned away, hating herself and him for her weakness, her voice shaking as she said quietly, 'I'll make some coffee. You will have a cup before you leave, won't you?'

'It won't work, Maggie. Try as you may, you won't always be able to turn your back on me. You know in your heart that you want me.'

She glanced back at him, standing poised in the doorway so that the pale wintry sunlight flooding along the hall caught her, turning her hair into a circle of fire around her head and turning the soft silk nightdress which lay like pale blue mist over her small high breasts almost transparent. 'You're wrong, Matthew. I don't want you!'

'No?' He smiled gently, moving just a few steps closer to her yet not attempting to touch her with his hands as he let his eyes drift over her. 'I hear what you're saying, Maggie, but can you blame me for not believing you when your body says something quite different?'

She looked down, following the line his eyes had taken, and sucked in a tiny gasping breath when she saw her rigid, swollen nipples pushing against the delicate fabric.

'See, Maggie? See how you can't hide your feelings, can't lie about what you want? You want me and there's nothing you can do about it.'

She shook her head, looking back at him with dread. 'There is! I...I won't let you come back into my life and destroy it again, Matthew. I won't!'

'I don't think you have that much choice. The fire is still there between us, still as hot and strong as ever, and one day all it will take is a look, a touch, and then it will start burning out of control again.' He laughed wryly, a strange expression on his face. 'I wish it weren't like that myself, but there's nothing either you or I can do about it!'

'There is!' Overcome by the need to convince him, she grasped his hand, holding it tightly with both of hers. 'You can stop this now, Matthew, before it goes any further and one of us gets hurt!'

He looked down, studying her hands curled around his, an odd expression of pain on his face. 'I can't stop it, Maggie. I only wish I could, that it was that easy! Every day since we parted I have prayed that I would wake up the next and not think of you, not feel this tearing ache in my gut, but it won't go. It's always there.'

'But what you are doing is wrong! You can't make yourself feel better by hurting me. It's...it's uncivilised!'

He laughed harshly, his eyes bitter. 'But isn't that what you taunted me with the other day, the fact that our relationship has never been civilised? What makes you think that it's going to suddenly change now?'

It was pointless trying to convince him, pointless to stand there any longer arguing. She let his hand go and turned away, her head bowed against the heavy pain that surged inside her. 'I'll just get a robe then make that coffee. I won't be long.'

'You could always help yourself, Maggie. Stop fighting me and let yourself enjoy what we are going to share. It would be no hardship, after all. And you are hardly the little innocent that you were when we met and married!'

She stopped dead as though he had struck her, her whole body tensing. What was he suggesting, that she should agree to have an affair with him? 'Never!' she spat back at him, her face filled with fury and contempt. 'Not even if hell freezes over will I ever agree to go back to you willingly!'

He laughed softly. 'Never is a long time, my sweet, but I'm quite prepared to wait. Whatever it takes, Maggie, however long, you will be mine again!'

She fled from the room, wanting only to set some distance between them before he saw how terrified she was, expecting to hear the sound of his laughter mocking her as she ran. But, strangely, there was only silence echoing in her wake, and for some reason that seemed to make her even more afraid.

The rich smell of coffee filled the kitchen when she came downstairs twenty minutes later, carefully

dressed in smart trousers and a heavy cream wool
sweater, with her hair drawn back from her face.
Matthew was standing by the counter, watching the
last drops of coffee drip into the glass jug. He
looked round when she walked into the room and
instinctively she stiffened, readying herself for yet
another verbal battle.

She had tried her hardest to regain her composure while she had showered and dressed, realising that it was the only way she could hope to
fight him. The passion of anger was so close to the
other sort of passion he could unleash in her that
she couldn't continue taking the risk. Standing
under the hot needles of water in the shower, she
had convinced herself yet again that the only way
to handle this was by staying calm and refusing to
be drawn into any further arguments. Now she
faced him with a cool hauteur, which was somewhat
wasted when he said blandly, 'There's toast on the
table and the coffee is just about ready. I may as
well pour it and save you the job.'

Maggie nodded briefly and sat down, wondering
if he had done that deliberately to throw her off
track. Well, if he had then it wouldn't work! She
knew Matthew too well to fall for any of his tricks!

'Still take it black, do you, or have you stopped
starving yourself as you used to do?'

He sat down opposite her, pouring coffee into
two china mugs before offering her the milk jug
with a quirk of his dark brow. Maggie took it from
him and poured a healthy measure of creamy milk
into the mug, watching the way the coffee marbled
as it sank into the hot liquid. Picking up the sugar
bowl, she added a small spoonful and stirred the

drink, then stared defiantly back at him. He laughed softly, picking up the jug to add milk to his own drink, his eyes gleaming with amusement.

'I should have tried that a couple of years back! I used to worry about the way you hardly ate a thing in case you put on an ounce of weight.'

'I didn't!' she snapped, then flushed when she met his steady gaze. 'Well, all right, then, so I was rather conscious of putting on any weight, but I never starved myself!'

'No? If I didn't know that it would only start another argument I would take you up on that, but I shall let it pass for now. I'm just glad to see that you have decided to be sensible rather than keep on making all those sacrifices for the sake of your job.'

It was the way he said it in that dismissing tone that annoyed her, reminding her of old hurts and grievances which had lain dormant in her mind too long, and she rounded on him, forgetting her decision to stay calm.

'You have always been the same, haven't you? Always resented my job and gone out of your way to pull it down.'

He looked almost startled for a moment before his eyes narrowed. 'Is it any wonder when you were so totally obsessed with it, almost to the exclusion of everything else?'

'That is not true! I gave up assignment after assignment when we were married just to keep you happy. Does that sound like something an obsessed person would do?'

He picked up the mug, his long fingers clenching around the fine bone china for a moment before he took a sip and made a deliberate effort to relax. 'The assignments you gave up, Maggie, were the ones you weren't really interested in. They were never the trips abroad or all over the country.'

'What difference does that make?'

'It made a lot of difference to me!' He set the mug down with a sharp clatter, a dangerous edge to his voice. 'I wanted you here, with me, Maggie, not off somewhere on the other side of the world!'

'Why? So that you could keep tabs on me, I suppose. Make sure that I wasn't chatting to any other man?'

'No, dammit, at least not at first. I missed you!'

'Oh.' She was so startled by the ferocity of the unexpected reply that she stared at him in silence.

He smiled bitterly. 'Does that shock you? It shouldn't. I was crazy about you, Maggie, from the first moment I set eyes on you. All I wanted was to have you with me, to make a life for us together. Heaven knows, I had never had much of a home life before that!'

'But your parents...David? You had a family, Matthew, and a home.'

'Yes, I had all those, on the surface. Hasn't David told you about our so-called home life?'

She shook her head, the coffee growing cold as she let it go untouched. 'He never mentions either you or your parents.'

'It's little wonder! We hardly saw either of them when we were children. Mother was always too busy with one or other of her good causes, while Father was totally immersed in the practice. He was a cold, hard man until the day he died. I doubt if he ever felt anything for anyone in the whole of his life.

Perhaps that was why he was so good at what he did. The law needs to be employed dispassionately, and my father was that sort of a person.'

'I never knew. I only met your father that one time at the wedding. I'd heard he had died a few months ago, of course. It was in all the papers, but even then David said very little about him. He went home for the funeral and stayed a few days with your mother, and then that was that.'

He nodded. 'I saw him then.'

'You did? But he never...' She tailed off, picking up the mug to take a sip of the half-cold drink.

'But he never mentioned that he had seen me? Is that what you were going to say?' He laughed harshly. 'I don't wonder! We hardly met on the best of terms, as you can imagine!'

'I wish you would try to sort things out between you both. It's stupid to continue fighting like this. You said you had no real home life; well, maybe you didn't, Matthew, but at least you know who your parents are, and where you come from. I never had the luxury of that!' She set the mug down, her hand shaking so that coffee slopped on to the table. 'Even my name isn't truly my own! Did you know that?' Her face closed up as she tried to contain the pain that had always lain in her heart. 'I was named Magdalena after the nun who cared for me, and Duncan after the man who found me in the convent garden. That is my heritage, Matthew. Two borrowed names!'

'Then why in heaven's name did you throw away what I was offering you?' Anger rippled in his deep voice. 'Did you just grow tired of me, Maggie, and want something or someone fresh? I've tried my

best to understand why you threw it all away, but
I can't. I can't!'

'I threw nothing away. You say that all you
wanted from me was to build a life together, but
that's not true. You wanted to own me, Matthew.
You wanted to dictate my life and have me run it
on your terms! I, too, wanted a home, but I didn't
know how to go about making one because I'd had
no experience to draw on. All I knew was life in
the children's home and then modelling. And yes,
my work was important to me because it was all I
had. It gave me an identity. People were actually
asking for me, taking notice of the fact that I did
exist, and you wanted to take that away from me
because you were too blinded by jealousy to see
that!' She stood up, unaware of the tears that were
falling from her eyes. 'I think you should leave now.
Thank you for staying the night, but I'm sure that
you need to get home now.'

He stood up, coming round the table to her and
barring her path when she tried to walk past him
and leave the room. 'You can't keep running away,
Maggie. It won't change anything. I shall keep on
coming back until I wear you down.'

'I won't let you in! I don't want you here!'

'Maybe not, but that won't stop me, nor will it
stop how we both feel.' He grasped her by the
shoulders, pulling her to him to hold her firmly
against the length of his body, and Maggie sup-
pressed a gasp of shock when she felt the hardness
of him pressed against her soft flesh.

Her eyes flew up to his, wide, startled, filled with
awareness, and he smiled slowly, easing her hips
closer and closer against him, moving her in a

steady rhythm which sent the heat scorching through her limbs.

'I met you, Maggie, and it was like a chain being forged, one link meshing with the next, and those links are still there, unbroken, as strong as they ever were. You will never be free of me... never!'

'No, I...' The denial died on her lips as he bent his head and took her mouth in a kiss that burnt with a raw, wild passion. Maybe if he had kissed her harshly then she could have fought him, could have found the strength from somewhere to make him stop, but she wasn't proof against this heady assault on her senses.

Time after time his mouth moved over hers, inviting a response she was powerless to deny him. Her mouth softened, clung, her lips parting to allow him to deepen the kiss, shuddering as his tongue swept round the soft inner recesses and tangled with hers. He groaned harshly, the rough sound sending a heady excitement curling through her in convulsive waves, so that when his hands slid up the smooth skin of her back under the soft warm folds of the thick sweater she made no protest.

'Maggie!' Her name was a whisper of sweet music, a prayer, an enchantment, said that way, and she felt her heart leap in sheer joy. She tugged at his shirt, easing the cotton fabric out of the waistband of his trousers so that she could slide her fingers over his warm skin, savouring the silken smoothness of his back, the faint abrasive rub of hair across his chest. He shuddered violently, his big body convulsing in a spasm of pleasure and need which brought a surge of tenderness into her heart.

He needed her, needed her touch to make him whole again.

When his hands slid round her to the underside of her breasts she moaned softly, her body tensing as she waited for the touch of his fingers against her flesh.

'Do you want me, Maggie? Do you?' His voice was a delicious ripple of sound, warm and deep, and she shivered in pleasure.

'Yes. Yes, Matthew!'

'Want me so much that you ache?'

What was he doing? Why was he talking like that? Her eyes slid open, the lids heavy over the passion-drugged emerald depths, and she frowned in confusion. His hands tightened around her, his fingers brushing the soft ripe swell of her breasts just for a moment before he slowly, deliberately set her away from him.

'So now you know exactly what it feels like to want someone almost to the point of madness. Remember how it feels. Get used to living with that ache just as quickly as you can, because it's going to be with you now, day after day, night after night!'

He stepped back, tucking the shirt neatly back into place, his movements steady and precise, betraying no hint of that shuddering need she'd felt in him before, and that more than anything brought her back to her senses.

It had been a trick, a cruel, deliberate trick to teach *her* a lesson and make *him* feel better. What a fool she was, what a mindless, trusting fool!

Cold waves of humiliation filled her and she turned away, missing the sudden pain which crossed his face as he studied her downbent head. Just for a second he seemed to hesitate, before he drew himself together and his expression hardened. He left the room, lifting his jacket off the hall peg before going from the house without a backward glance.

Maggie heard him leave, but it was a long time before she looked up, her face a stark mask of grief. He had hurt her before, so in a way she should be used to it, should be able to deal with the pain now, but she couldn't.

She still loved him. Somewhere during that brief moment of madness she had suddenly realised the fact, and now it struck fear into her heart as she acknowledged it. Her only hope now lay in never letting him find out.

CHAPTER SIX

'WHO'D be a model? If anyone dares say to me ever again what a glamorous job it is then I'll . . . I'll scream!'

Marie hurried into the trailer, slamming the door against a blast of cold air before huddling down in front of the Calor gas heater. Maggie moved aside, smiling wryly as she lifted a thick mohair shawl off the back of the chair and handed it to her friend.

'You mean to tell me that you don't *enjoy* standing out there in the middle of a gale almost naked? Tut, tut, my dear, and you call yourself a professional!'

Marie glowered at her as she snatched the shawl and wrapped it around her bare shoulders. 'Too right I do! No one but a professional model would put up with conditions like that! Whose brilliant idea was this anyway? Give me a gun and I'll happily shoot him.'

Maggie laughed. 'Still feel the same if I tell you that Denis thought this all up? He felt the stark contrast of the derelict buildings and the evening gowns would cause maximum impact.'

'I should have known. That man is crazy.' There was little amusement in Marie's tone as she stared into the glowing heat of the fire, and Maggie felt a stirring of sympathy.

'Still not got things properly sorted out between you, then? I thought you'd succeeded the other night when you went round to his flat.'

'So did I, but it didn't take long for it all to get unsorted, believe me. What is it with men, Maggie? Why do they always manage to mix your life up and complicate things?'

Maggie shrugged, her face clouded as she slipped off the heavy quilted jacket which looked oddly at variance with the elegance of the full-skirted black velvet evening gown. 'Don't ask me. I'm no authority at all on men!'

Marie swivelled round, ignoring the fact that she was crushing the filmy skirt of the expensive gown. 'Want to tell me about it, Mags? That was your ex-husband at your house the other night, wasn't it?'

'Yes.' Maggie picked up the hairbrush from the assortment spread along the laminated counter which served as a make-up bench, and ran it through her glossy hair.

'Are you planning on getting back together again or what? I felt such a fool walking in like that and finding you both in that clinch. I used to think that you and David were an item, but I soon gave that idea up after I'd seen you together a couple of times, although I have the feeling that David might like the relationship to be more along those lines.'

Maggie's hand shook as she set the brush down, staring at her friend with worried eyes. 'Do you think so? Oh, I hope not! I don't need that sort of complication just now.' She drew in a sharp breath, willing herself to stay calm, but it was a struggle when her nerves were already stretched so thin. It had been over a week now since Matthew had stayed the night at her house, and she'd not heard a word from him, but the shock was still there about what he had done and what she had discovered about her feelings for him. She felt as if she was on a tightrope, balanced precariously over a chasm into which she might fall at any minute. She had tried to keep going for Janey's sake, sticking rigidly to her daily routine, but it would be so hard to do that if she lost the support from David that she had come to rely on so desperately. Yet she couldn't bear the thought of hurting him by letting him fall in love with her.

'I know the divorce must have been rough on you, Maggie, but are you sure that you don't still care about Matthew?' Marie looked down at her exquisitely manicured nails, missing the shock that showed on Maggie's face. 'You could have cut the tension in the room with a knife the other night, and I don't mean that it was anger! It's obvious that the chemistry is still there between you both, so isn't it worth taking a second shot at a life together . . . especially for Janey's sake?'

'What do you mean?' Maggie swung round in alarm, her face going ashen, and Marie jumped to her feet.

'Nothing! Look, I'm sorry. I didn't mean to upset you. Come on, sit down.' She tried to ease Maggie over to the chair set against the wall, but Maggie shrugged her off.

'I'm fine. I don't need to sit down. What did you mean about Janey? She has nothing whatsoever to do with Matthew . . . nothing!'

Her voice was shrill, and Marie studied her in concern before slowly shaking her head. 'You know that isn't true, Maggie. Janey is his daughter, isn't she?'

Where was the point in lying? 'Yes.' The word whispered brokenly from her, and Marie grimaced, taking her hand to hold it tightly.

'Does he know?'

'No! And he mustn't . . . ever!'

'Don't worry, I won't say anything. But some day soon someone else is going to notice the resemblance. She's the image of him.'

'I know.' She forced a shaky smile, easing her hand away. 'Ridiculous, isn't it? But as far as Matthew is concerned she is David's child, and that's what I want him to go on thinking.'

'Well, he won't hear differently from me, I promise you that. But have you really thought what you are doing, Maggie? Are you sure that you're right to keep it from him that he has a daughter? And are you sure that you have the right to deny Janey her father? It's one heck of a big decision to be responsible for taking.'

There was genuine concern in Marie's liquid-dark eyes for a moment before she picked up the heap of outdoor clothing from the back of the chair. 'Well, I'd better go and get changed. My stint out there in the Arctic is over, thank heavens. It's all yours now, kiddo . . . enjoy!'

She disappeared into the tiny changing area at the rear of the cluttered trailer, and Maggie turned back to the mirror, picking up a brush to dust blusher over her pale cheeks and across the smooth sweep of her forehead. She studied herself in the brightly lit glass, staring into eyes which were dark with fear, their emerald depths now the colour of a stormy sea. All along she had known that at some point someone would see the resemblance between Janey and Matthew, but she'd hoped and prayed that it wouldn't be for many years if Matthew remained out of the country. Now she had to face the fact that it had happened and could happen again now that he was back and intent on being part of her life for however short a time. Surely it would be better all round to tell him and get it over and done with?

'Are you ready, Maggie? We're waiting for you.'

She jumped when Claire, the stylist working on the assignment, banged on the trailer door, dropping the brush so that a fine cloud of creamy-pink blusher rose in the air, veiling her reflection with a delicate tinted mist, and she sighed. She had long since stopped looking at life through rose-tinted spectacles and she wasn't going to be fool enough to start doing so again at her age. If Matthew ever found out about Janey then he would never rest in his quest for revenge. It was a fact, and there was little point in trying to convince herself otherwise.

The wind was sharp as she stepped out of the trailer and made her way across to where Denis was waiting, warmly dressed in a fur-trimmed parka. He grinned when he saw her approaching, ignoring the spiky look she gave him as she took up position next to the derelict building.

'I know, love. I know. Marie has said it all before. But this is going to be one hell of a set of pictures, Mags, and the fee will make it all worthwhile.'

Maggie shivered. 'It had better!'

'It will, it will,' he said soothingly, turning back to his camera. 'Now remember what we worked out before. I want you to try looking sad, a little bit lonely.' He studied her fine, delicate features for a second. 'It shouldn't be difficult to get what I'm after; there's a haunting quality about you already.'

They worked on the shots for almost thirty minutes, Maggie adopting pose after pose, blocking the discomfort of the cold wind from her mind as she always did once she started working. A model's main asset apart from her beauty was a strong constitution, and she had been blessed with that. It had meant that she had been able to shake off that heavy cold she'd had, although it was barely a week since it had reached its peak. However, she was more than glad when Denis announced that he was satisfied. Good constitution or not, another ten minutes or so and she would have been flirting with pneumonia.

She ran back to the trailer, shivering violently as the warmth hit her, but she wasted no more than a minute getting warm in front of the heater before hurrying through to the back to get changed into her customary jeans and sweater. Leaving the expensive gown hanging on the rail, she creamed off the heavy make-up, smiling her thanks when Marie brought her a mug of steaming tea.

'Here, this should thaw you out.'

'Thanks.' She took a tentative sip, then set the mug down to brush her hair and catch it back from her face in a plain tortoiseshell clip. 'So what's happening now? Do you want a lift back into town with me?'

'If you don't mind. There's no point in . . .' She broke off with colour running up her cheeks when Denis opened the trailer door and stuck his head inside.

'Have you got a minute, Marie? I need to talk to you,' he asked tersely.

Marie's mouth tightened mutinously, the refusal visibly hovering on her lips, and Maggie piped up quickly.

'Of course she has.'

Marie gave her a venomous look then followed Denis outside, and Maggie sighed as she stood up and went to pack her case. Why was love always such a tricky emotion to handle? Why could it never just flow smoothly into the happy-ever-after one read about in books?

There was no answer to either question, of course, so she worked away until the door suddenly opened again and Marie reappeared, looking unusually flustered. 'Well?'

'Do you mind if I don't have that lift, after all? Denis has offered to take me home.'

Maggie smiled, mentally crossing her fingers for both her friends. 'Of course I don't. Off you go.'

Marie rushed off and she got back to her packing, finally getting it all done by the time Claire hurried in, obviously eager to call it a day. She left the trailer, pulling the collar of the quilted jacket around her ears as she walked over to where her car was parked.

Denis had chosen this location out of several likely ones around the city mainly because there was a strangely barren beauty about the crumbling Victorian warehouses overlooking the grey swell of

the winter river. There was a tang of moisture in
the cold air, combined with the faint sweet odour
of rotting vegetation, and Maggie paused to inhale
the unfamiliar scents while she enjoyed the solitude.
The sudden noisy roar of the trailer's engine broke
the silence and she glanced round to wave to Claire,
who was sitting next to the driver, then unlocked
the door of her car and dropped the heavy case on
to the back seat with a sigh. So much for solitude:
now it was time to head back to the fray, and first
on the agenda was a visit to the supermarket, closely
followed by collecting Janey from the sitter.

She slid behind the wheel and turned the ignition, cursing silently when nothing happened
apart from a small whine. The starter motor had
been playing up for a couple of days now and the
car was booked into the garage to be checked the
following morning. Please heaven it wasn't going
to be a nuisance now!

She tried several more times to start the car but
the only response each time was that irritating
whine, and she slapped her hand against the
steering-wheel in disgust. Why did it have to happen
here? The dock was huge, and the part of it that
Denis had chosen to use was at the furthermost end,
a good mile away from the road.

She got out of the car and hefted the heavy case
off the back seat, unwilling to leave it behind.
Although the whole complex appeared deserted,
there was no knowing who might come along and
be tempted to break into the car to steal the case.
It had taken her years to collect the items in her
"bag of tricks", not to mention the mind-boggling
cost of the make-up.

Locking the door, she set off across the dockside, keeping a wary eye open for any broken flags. The site was scheduled for renovation within the year to turn the derelict warehouses into riverfront apartments, but little had been done for years now, so the ground was treacherously uneven. The last thing she needed was a twisted ankle to add to her woes.

'And what have you got there, little lady?'

She stifled a scream, jumping back in alarm as a shabby figure stepped out from one of the doorways and confronted her. The man gestured at the case, smiling in a way that sent fear scudding up her spine. He was roughly dressed in a torn overcoat, fastened round his waist with string, and a filthy woollen hat pulled down low over his ears. He was heavily bearded so that she could see little of his face apart from his eyes, but that was enough. Glazed, almost feverishly bright, they fastened greedily on her as he moved forward, and Maggie looked frantically round.

He laughed out loud, the sound rising and falling on the still, sharp air, strangely high-pitched and unnatural, and her fear intensified.

'There's no one here but you and me, lady, so don't bother looking for help. Now just give me that nice big bag while I see what you've got in there.'

He made a grab for the case but instinctively Maggie snatched it away, almost gagging at the sour smell of filth and alcohol which wafted off him.

'Get away!' she shouted. 'Don't you dare touch me!' She swung the case wildly, catching him a lucky blow on his side so that he staggered, and that was all she needed. She rushed past him, running for all she was worth across the dockyard, almost sobbing in fear. She raced round a corner, then screamed when she cannoned into someone, struggling wildly as she felt hands fasten on her shoulders. Her flailing hands beat at the air before connecting with flesh, and she raked her nails down the person's face before suddenly, shockingly realising that someone was shouting her name.

'Maggie, it's me...stop it! Damn you woman, stop that!' Her arms were crushed to her sides, effectively stopping her from struggling, and for the first time she actually looked at who was holding her and gasped in astonishment.

'Matthew! How...why...? I... Ohhh!' Suddenly it was all too much and she fell against him, clinging tightly hold of him as though she never wanted to let him go. He held her in silence as he smoothed a hand over her hair, his tall body deliciously familiar and reassuring, until slowly the shuddering gasps of fear abated.

'Tell me what happened. What are you doing here and why were you running like that?' His deep voice was such a comfort, and she gave a tiny little gasp of relief and laughter.

'Am I glad that you were here? There was this man, you see...' She started to look back over her shoulder then yelped in pain as his hands contracted on her arms.

'What man? Did you come here with someone and he got out of hand? Is that what you're saying?'

Fury contorted his face and she dragged herself free, staring at him with eyes glazed with pain. 'Of course not!'

He seemed to make an effort to regain control
but his voice was still edged with steel. 'Then what
the hell are you doing here in this godforsaken spot?
And where is this man you spoke of?' He looked
past her, but the dockyard was deserted now, only
the sound of the dry clumps of weeds blowing in
the wind breaking the silence. Maggie forced herself
to be calm, to keep the pain of that cruel accusation from tearing her apart.

'I was here working on an assignment. My car
wouldn't start when I tried it and, seeing as
everyone else had already gone, I started walking
back to the road. The . . . the man just jumped out
in front of me and tried to snatch my case.'

There was a lingering echo of fear in her voice
and Matthew swore roughly, pushing her aside to
walk back several yards the way she'd come before
he came back again, his face grim. 'There doesn't
appear to be any sign of him now. You've had a
lucky escape, but it beats me why you didn't just
give him the damned case rather than risk getting
yourself hurt! What have you got in there, the
crown jewels?'

The cold sarcasm stung and she glared at him.
'Very funny, but no. It's just my make-up and stuff
like that.'

'And you consider that worth fighting for?' He
raised a disbelieving brow.

'Frankly, yes! But I wouldn't expect you to
understand!' She turned on her heel, terrified of
doing something desperate, like slapping his
mocking face, if she had to listen a moment longer.

'And where do you think you're going?' He caught her arm and stopped her, his fingers tightening when she tried to shake him off.

'Home, of course. Now please let me go!'

He released her at once and stepped back. 'Certainly, if that's what you really want.'

She stared at him suspiciously. This wasn't like Matthew, to give up so readily. What was he playing at now?

With a worried little glance at his calm face, she set off again, expecting any second to have him stop her, but he made no attempt to do that. She looked back over her shoulder uncertainly, her footsteps slowing when she saw the way he was watching her with a faint smile on his face and his arms folded easily over his broad chest. He was dressed quite formally today in a heavy navy overcoat over a navy pin-striped suit, clothing which should have looked ridiculously out of place in the dockside setting, but it didn't seem to matter what he was wearing. He looked tough and uncompromising, as she knew to her cost he was: so why was he letting her do exactly what she chose to for once?

'Oh, Maggie.' There was just the tiniest hint of amusement in his beautiful voice as it carried on the wind to where she stood hesitating, and she stiffened in readiness.

'What?'

'Have you stopped to consider the fact that your assailant is unlikely to be here alone? In my experience, docks like this are a haunt for any number of tramps and vagrants. So how do you think you'll fare if you meet up with a group of them along the way?'

'I...' She looked round, her heart leaping un-
comfortably as she spotted what could be
movement in the shadows cast by the building a
few yards away, but something inside her refused
to back down. 'I'll manage. Don't concern yourself
on my account, Matthew!'

He shrugged easily, smoothing a hand over the
windswept darkness of his hair. 'Fair enough.
Please yourself.'

He turned away, walking briskly in the opposite
direction, and Maggie took a couple of faltering
steps after him.

'Where are you going?'

He barely managed to spare her a glance over his
shoulder. 'Back to my car, of course. There's no
point in hanging around here in the cold. I'll see
you some time, I expect.' He nodded briefly then
set off again, his long legs eating up the distance.
Maggie glanced round a little wildly before her eyes
slid back to the patch of shadow and her heart leapt
afresh in fear. There *was* someone there...she was
sure of it now!

'Matthew, stop! Wait for me.' She thought he
hadn't heard her because he kept on walking, and
she started to run, the case banging painfully against
her legs. He slowed when she came alongside him,
gasping for breath, her eyes flashing with annoyance. 'Didn't you hear me calling you?' she
demanded.

He smiled almost gently. 'Yes, I heard all right,
but I just wanted to make certain that you really
had changed your mind.'

There was something in his voice, something
which made her go hot all over, and her face suf-

fused with angry colour. 'About the lift, that's all!
I haven't changed my mind about anything else!'

'No?' He raised a dark brow, taking the case
from her hand as though it weighed nothing. 'Well,
let's just see that as an encouraging sign that you
aren't entirely intractable. If you can change your
mind once, Maggie, then who knows if you will
change it again and realise that what I said the other
day made good sense? An affair would be the
perfect way to get all this out of both our systems.'

'But an affair isn't just what you want, is it,
Matthew? You want revenge, and I won't be stupid
enough to put myself in that sort of position...ever.'

'We'll see, I expect.'

'We won't *see* anything!' Her temper bubbled
over and she shouted back at him, but he appeared
infuriatingly unmoved as he started walking again.

'Never, Matthew. Never...never...never!'

It was the wind, of course, catching the sound
of her voice and tossing it playfully about. Why
else should it have sounded more like a plea than
a denial?

The car was a haven of warmth and comfort, and
despite herself Maggie relaxed into the softness of
the leather seat while Matthew drove across the city.
He handled the huge, powerful car as he handled
everything else, with a skill and expertise which
made little of the heavy traffic. Nothing ever seemed
to prick that in-built composure, not even her obvious displeasure, and she gnawed at her lip, feeling
the worry nagging away inside her. How could she
ever hope to be a match for him when he outwitted
her at every turn?

The car slid to a halt and she looked round blankly at the elegant house set in a terraced row of similar houses where they had stopped. 'Where are we?'

'My house.'

'Your house? But why have we come here? Look, Matthew, if this is another of your little tricks then let me——'

He cut her off. 'I have to collect some papers that I need for a meeting later on tonight. That's why I've brought you back here, plus the fact that there is no way I can go back to chambers like this.'

He turned his head and she stifled a gasp as she saw the angry scratches down the side of his cheek. Several were obviously quite deep and encrusted with blood. She half reached out to touch them before snatching her hand back with guilty haste. 'Did I really do that?'

Mockery crossed his face as he leant back in his seat and studied the guilt etched on her face. 'Don't you recognise your own handiwork, then? After all, it isn't the first time that you've left your mark on me, Maggie.'

Heat ran along her veins like bush fire and she turned away to stare out of the window, remembering the other times when he had roused her to such mindless passion that she'd been unaware of raking her nails down his back. He laughed quietly but said nothing while he slid the key from the ignition and opened the car door. 'Aren't you coming, then?'

She shook her head, keeping her attention centred on the row of houses as though she found the view enthralling.

'No? And here I was, hoping that you would at least agree to clean these cuts, seeing as you are responsible for them. I've never particularly relished the sight of blood.'

His voice was quite bland, but she turned and shot him a venomous look. Since when did he have any trouble with the sight of blood? He was just trying to play upon her guilt, and it wouldn't work!

'Surely you're not afraid to come inside, not when you are so completely certain that I'll never get a hold on you again?'

It was a taunting challenge and she reacted to it with an impetuosity she immediately regretted. 'Of course I'm not!'

'Then there's no problem, is there?'

He climbed out and came round to hold the door for her, leaving her little option but to get out or cause a scene, and she wouldn't give him the satisfaction of doing that!

She stepped out of the car, glaring at his broad back as she followed him up the steep steps and in through the front door. While he took his overcoat off she stared round the elegant hallway, reluctantly admiring the pale satin-stripe paper and exquisite Chinese rugs strewn across the polished hard-wood floor.

'So, what do you think?'

She shrugged, annoyed that he had found her looking round with such interest, as though it *mattered* to her where and how he lived. 'It's very nice. I'm surprised that you have managed to get everything so perfect in only a few weeks.'

'Oh, I've had the house far longer than that. I bought it soon after I sold the other one, and have kept it ready for whenever I decided to move back to England. I have an excellent housekeeper who runs everything for me.'

He led the way along the hall, mercifully missing her shocked expression. She had had no idea that all the time she'd been thinking he was safely out of the way in America he had been planning to come back some day! Would she have slept easy at night if she'd known of his plans? She doubted it, and suddenly realised just how naïve she'd been to assume that Matthew would quietly fade away because that was what she wanted.

'Why don't you take a good look round the place while I get my things together? I've a few phone calls as well that I need to make, so take your time. Mrs Davies, my housekeeper, is away at present, so there's no one here apart from us.'

She would have liked to refuse just to show how little she cared about his home, but the thought of having to sit waiting patiently while he collected his things was more than she could face. She wandered down the rest of the long hall as he disappeared into what was evidently a study, peering into the beautifully decorated rooms. The house was so different from the one they had shared that she found herself lingering in the doorway to the sitting-room, wondering if he had deliberately chosen the light airy colour schemes for the same reasons she had done. What irony!

'Like it?'

She hadn't heard him approaching and she spun round, putting out a hand to steady herself as she almost overbalanced. Her fingers slid inside the open front of his suit jacket and she felt her breath

catch as she felt the heavy thud of his heart under
her palm. Just for a moment her hand lingered
against the warm hardness of his flesh beneath the
thin white shirt before she snatched it away.

'It's lovely. A beautiful room. Did you get
someone in to choose the colour scheme and furniture, or did you do it all yourself?'

She was gabbling, she could hear herself, the
words rushing in a torrent from her lips, and he
smiled almost gently as he pressed a long finger
against her mouth to halt the frantic flow.

'Does it shock you, Maggie, that you can still
feel this way even though you claim to hate me so
much?'

She backed away from him, her eyes huge and
frantic. 'No! If you think you're going to start that
again then I'm leaving now!'

He shook his head, studying her flushed face with
curiously flat eyes. 'There's no need. This is hardly
the time to start yet another endless repetition of
what's already been said. I've got everything I need,
so if you'd just do something about these scratches
then we can leave.'

He led the way along the hall to the kitchen,
leaving her standing in the doorway while he crossed
the room to open one of the tall oak cupboards and
lift out a bottle of antiseptic and a roll of cotton
wool.

Maggie waited until he had sat down at the
kitchen table, then shrugged off her coat and tossed
it over a chair with an outward composure that
didn't reach very deep. He always managed to un-
settle her, always managed to make her so *aware*

of him, so that even this seemingly harmless act of cleaning the scratches took on a greater significance.

Her hand shook as she tore a piece off the cotton wool and soaked it in antiseptic before smoothing it tentatively down the angry marks on his face. He winced sharply and she felt a ripple of regret for having injured him this way, before deliberately hardening her heart. She bent down and cleansed the cuts, searching for something to say to break the tension that seemed to fill the room.

'You never did tell me what you were doing at the docks.'

'I never had a chance!' There was a faint edge to his voice, which she ignored, determined to keep the peace, and after a moment he continued.

'I was there to meet someone who had some information I need. He suggested the dock as being the one place where we wouldn't be interrupted or seen together.'

'I see. It seems all very cloak and dagger to me.'

He shrugged. 'It probably does, but it was necessary. Two witnesses have met with nasty accidents already on this case, and we can't afford to have a third.'

Her hand stilled and she frowned. 'What sort of accidents?'

'Ones that were just too coincidental to be true.' He sighed roughly. 'You've probably heard about that bullion robbery.'

'Yes.'

'Well, my father was acting as defence for one of the men charged with stealing the gold. He has turned Queen's evidence in exchange for the promise of a lenient sentence. However, his friends aren't too keen that he should get off while they get gaoled. There have been several attempts to intimidate the jury, plus those accidents, and that was before the trial had to be postponed when Father died. I have taken over the case from him.'

'It sounds dangerous.'

'No more dangerous than many another case that I've been involved in. Have you finished yet?'

'What?' For a moment she didn't understand what he meant, swamped by quite unexpected concern that he might be in danger.

'My face. Will it do?'

'Oh, yes.' She summoned up a thin smile to hide her feelings. 'You had better be prepared for a few comments, though. Those marks are very obviously scratches. Perhaps you can claim that a cat made them.'

'A cat . . . or a tigress? I think the latter is a more apt description, don't you?'

His voice was so deep that it shivered against her skin like velvet, and she bit back a gasp. 'Matthew, I don't think that . . .'

His hand slid around the back of her neck, his fingers burrowing into her hair to release the clasp so that it tumbled in rich silken waves around her face. 'That's always been your trouble, Maggie— you think too much.'

He drew her head down, kissing her parted lips lightly, his mouth barely brushing against the warm soft contours of hers, before he pulled away. 'Why do you always keep on snatching your hair back like this? I've dreamt about it tumbling round your shoulders like this, dreamt about waking up and seeing it spread like fire over the pillow as you lie next to me.'

He was doing it again, using his voice and the images he could draw in her head to snare her back into that heady enchantment, and suddenly, shockingly, she didn't have the strength left to fight him.

Something must have shown on her face because he made a rough sound deep in his throat as he pulled her back to him and kissed her with such tenderness that tears filled her eyes.

'I've missed you, Maggie, missed you so much...wanted you so much.'

There was an ache of sadness in his deep, beautiful voice that cut her to the quick, and her arms slid around his neck to draw his head against the soft curve of her breasts in an instinctive act of comfort. Under her fingertips she felt his pulse leap, felt the rhythm of his blood start to beat in a furious tempo that was immediately echoed by her own. When he turned his face to nuzzle his lips against her breasts through the soft folds of the sweater she made no attempt to stop him, but drew him even closer, feeling the hot moistness of his breath clouding through the wool on to her skin.

'Lord, aren't you wearing anything under this?'

There was shocked disbelief in his voice, and she laughed softly, enjoying the very obvious effect the discovery of her nakedness had on him, enjoying being a woman, holding the man she loved in her arms.

'No,' she whispered, her voice filled with an invitation she knew he would understand.

When his hands slid under the hem of the sweater and lifted it she closed her eyes, shuddering at the

hot, faintly abrasive sweep of his tongue against
her aching flesh. It was madness to let this happen,
sheer undiluted folly, yet she was powerless against
the overwhelming need to have him love her.

Time after time his mouth worshipped each small
breast, his teeth grazing against the rigid nipples
until she felt so weak that she could barely stand.
He must have sensed how she felt because he stood
up, lifting the sweater over her head in one smooth
action to let his eyes feast on the pale cream and
mauve of her skin with a hunger that set a tremble
coursing along her limbs.

'You're so beautiful, Maggie. So very, very
beautiful.' His voice was husky with desire and she
closed her eyes, letting every hot, rich nuance warm
her and chase away three years of coldness from
her heart.

Surely it couldn't only be revenge he wanted?
Surely no one could fake that yearning need? There
must be some way to work things out. To have
Matthew love her again in every sense of the word
would be all of heaven, and worth taking any risk
for.

When he bent and lifted her into his arms she
slid her arm around his neck and drew his head
down to kiss him with an open-mouthed aban-
donment that made him shudder in response. He
drew back slowly, his eyes glazed, his breath coming
in heavy, laboured spasms as his broad chest rose
and fell against the soft swell of her breasts. 'Oh,
Maggie, you'll have me on my knees if you keep
that up!'

She laughed, arching her back to let her breasts
brush the hard wall of his chest, feeling his arms

contract almost helplessly as he carried her from
the kitchen and along the hall. Burrowing her face
against his neck, she bit delicately at the strong
cords, then let the moist tip of her tongue slide
down from the curve of his ear to where that pulse
was beating almost out of control.

He set her down abruptly, pulling her against him
almost violently to let her feel the unmistakable
evidence of his need before starting to lower her to
the floor. Her eyes opened, wide, startled, and he
smiled with a wry self-mocking humour as he slid
his hand down from her neck to the waistband of
her jeans.

'I don't think I can make it upstairs to the
bedroom, Maggie. You've got me as wound up as
a boy out on his first date.'

Her heart turned over at the helpless throb in his
voice, and she held her arms out to enfold him when
he followed her down to the rug. Their lovemaking
had always been passionate and frenzied, but never
like this. Matthew had always been in control
before, always able to keep a rein on his responses
as he had drawn her deeper and deeper into the
tides of passion. Now that control had snapped and
his vulnerability touched a hidden core in her,
making her love him even more.

His hands shook as he unfastened the snap on
her jeans and started to slide the zip down, and
Maggie twisted restlessly. All her senses seemed to
be heightened, so that just the gentle brush of his
fingers against her flesh filled her with fire, just the
sound of his harsh breathing made her shudder with
exquisite tension for what was to come. The world
had narrowed to this time and space that they

shared, so that when a clock suddenly chimed, intruding on that world, she jumped and turned her head to stare at it with passion-clouded eyes.

Three o'clock.

The chimes seemed to beat into her consciousness as she stared at the white face of the dial, wondering what was so important about the time.

Janey! She had to collect Janey from the sitter at three o'clock! How could she have forgotten that? How could she have forgotten Janey at all?

She started to struggle, pushing at Matthew's chest just as eagerly as she had drawn him to her only moments before.

'No. Please, Matthew. I'm sorry, but I have to go.'

'Go?' He repeated the word, his eyes unfocused, glazed, before they cleared with an abruptness that chilled her to the bone. He pushed himself away from her and stood up, staring down at her with a biting contempt all over his face. 'Go? Where?'

Maggie swallowed hard, feeling the bitter waves of anguish and cooling passion running along her veins, terrified all of a sudden to tell him why she had so suddenly changed her mind. 'Home.'

'Home. A bit sudden, this decision to go home, isn't it?' He ran his eyes down the length of her where she lay on the rug, and Maggie struggled to get up, wanting only to shield herself from the contempt she could see on his face.

'I'm sorry, Matthew. I really am, but I . . . I just remembered something important.'

'Important!' His anger erupted in a huge tidal wave, sucking them into its depths, and in her heart she knew she couldn't blame him. When he bent and caught her chin to lift her face to meet his blistering gaze she closed her eyes in mute defence.

'What, pray, is so important that you have to leave now for?'

There was no way she could avoid it now, no way that she could avoid the one answer which she knew was going to enrage him to an even greater fury. 'I have to collect Janey from the sitter at three o'clock. I'm sorry, Matthew...really sorry. I...I just forgot all about it.'

His whole body went rigid, the fingers clamped around her chin biting deep into the flesh before he thrust her from him and turned his back. Maggie scrambled to her feet and ran back to the kitchen, dragging the sweater over her head, suddenly ashamed of her nakedness and what it meant. She snatched up her coat and turned to go, stopping when she found Matthew standing in the doorway, one clenched fist resting against the door-frame. At some point during those frenzied moments of passion they had shared he had shed his suit jacket and unbuttoned his shirt so that it hung open, exposing the strong bare expanse of hair-roughened muscle to her faltering eyes. Her stomach lurched with a wild surge of remembered passion, and she looked away, not yet proof against such a sight.

'Congratulations, Maggie. I must admit that I had no idea that you could be such a devastating opponent when you choose. Has this evened the score for you?'

'I have no idea what you mean.' She didn't want to look at him and see how easily all that passion had turned to bitterness again, but with him standing there blocking the doorway she had little option. 'Look, Matthew, I've told you that I'm sorry. You must understand that I can't stay.'

'Of course you can't. Not when your daughter needs you so much. Was that the final thrust to embed the knife just that bit deeper, using her as your excuse to suddenly discover that you had to leave?'

'No! I didn't plan what happened. How could I have? I didn't *know* that we were coming back here!' She drew in a shuddering breath, willing herself to stay calm. 'I forgot all about having to collect Janey until I realised the time.'

'As I too almost forgot about her, but that wouldn't be the right thing to do, would it? To forget about your and David's child?'

His contempt rankled, making her forget caution for a moment. 'She isn't his . . .!' She broke off abruptly, appalled at what she had been about to say, and he laughed bitterly.

'Isn't what, Maggie, darling? Isn't David's? What a surprise! And just who is her father, then? Or don't you know? I should imagine it would be hard to select one man out of your legion of past lovers!'

'Why, you . . .!' Her hand shot out to slap his face, but he caught her wrist in an iron grip and hauled her against his body, subduing her with an ease that was galling.

'Don't do that, Maggie. I have never hit a woman in my life but I could very easily make an exception for you!' He flung her from him, watching as she stumbled back against the table. 'Now get out. I shall chalk this up to experience and from now on treat you with the respect you deserve as a cunning adversary. I had my turn the other day and now you have evened the score, so we're on equal footing from now on in, although I must warn you that I shall win.'

She had to convince him that it hadn't been deliberate, that she hadn't set out to lead him on and then reject him so cruelly. 'You're wrong...wrong! I didn't do it on purpose to pay you back or even any score. I just forgot!'

His lip curled in derision. 'So you keep saying, and maybe you did, for a moment or two, as I did. But believe me, Maggie, I won't forget again. That child is living proof of your deceit and there won't be a single minute in a single day that I will ever forget about her again!'

There was nothing she could say, no words that would convince him now apart from the truth, and she doubted that he would believe that.

She ran from the room, ran from the house, ran from the cold accusation in his eyes: ran and ran until she could run no further, but she couldn't run away from the pain that was tearing her apart.

CHAPTER SEVEN

'I TOLD you they'd be good, didn't I, Maggie? Worth every single frozen minute!'

There was a deep satisfaction on Denis's face as he held up one of the glossy prints for her inspection. 'Just take a look at that.'

Maggie looked, then slowly, almost reluctantly, nodded her agreement. The photograph of her in the dockland setting wearing the beautiful ballgown had a very special quality that immediately drew the eye. It seemed to tell a story, hint at emotions in a way that surprised even her.

Had she really looked so wistful that day, or had it been the angle that Denis had photographed her from? Suddenly it made her feel uncomfortable to see herself like that, as though the camera had captured a part of her that she had never intended it to.

She took the print from his hand and pretended to study it more closely, before slipping it to the bottom of the pile spread on the desk. 'They are really good, Denis. Is the client pleased with them?'

'Very much so. He phoned this morning, asking for details of which agency you and Marie are with so that he can arrange some sort of a forerunner to these appearing in the magazine. I explained that you were freelance, so he asked if you would give him a call to discuss it.'

'What kind of a forerunner? Did he say?'

Denis shrugged, gathering the photographs carefully together to slip them back into a stiffened folder. 'He didn't go into much detail, but I gathered it had something to do with that evening charity show next week. I think he was hoping that you would agree to model that gown there.'

'I don't usually do evening work if I can help it. I never like leaving Janey.'

'Well, it's up to you, of course, but I know he's very keen on the idea and that it could lead to some very lucrative work in the future. He's rapidly coming up in the fashion world and will be a name to watch before too long. He was particularly impressed by what he termed your "haunting quality".'

'I suppose I shall have to give him a ring and discuss it, but do you think he would be satisfied if Marie agreed to go even if I can't?'

'He might, but, seeing as Marie has taken herself off somewhere, that doesn't seem likely to happen!'

There was a harsh note in his voice and Maggie stared at him in surprise. 'Gone off? Where?'

'I've no idea. She didn't bother to tell me where. But she did say that she would ring you before she left, although it doesn't surprise me that she seems to have changed her mind. She has a habit of doing that!'

Denis picked up the folder and stormed out of the room, leaving Maggie staring after him in concern. It was obvious that he was upset, but what could she say in Marie's defence? She didn't want to have to start explaining that she'd made a point of not answering the telephone or the door when she'd been home. That would of necessity lead to more explanations as to why, and she didn't want to start discussing Matthew when she was trying her hardest to put him right out of her mind!

The changing-room was hot and crowded. Maggie elbowed her way into the small space allocated to her and set her case down, wishing she were anywhere but here. However, there had been no news from Marie, despite the fact that she had bought an answering machine to monitor any calls, so she had been forced to do the show tonight rather than let Denis and his client down.

It wasn't that she minded giving up her time for such a good cause, but she felt so guilty about leaving Janey at night when she had to leave her during the day. Of course, if her circumstances had been different and Janey had a father there to...

She cut off the thought, shocked that it should have slipped so easily into her head. Was her sub-consciousness trying to tell her something? If so, then what? To tell Matthew that he had a daughter, then sit back and hope that he would insist on playing happy families when he heard the news? The idea was farcical!

He had been unnervingly quiet for the last ten days or so since their disastrous meeting, but she wasn't foolish enough to believe that he had changed his mind. He was planning something, but the question was, what? She couldn't win: if he beat a constant path to her door that worried her, yet if he left her alone then that worried her even more! It was little wonder that her nerves were shot to threads.

An hour later she stood in the wings, waiting for her turn to take to the catwalk. If the enthusiastic applause was anything to go by then the evening had been a huge success so far. After the fashion parade there was dinner and dancing for the guests, who had paid a fortune for tickets to the prestigious event. Maggie had agreed to stay for the meal, but after that she would leave, not finding much attraction in the thought of staying the whole evening by herself.

The applause faded and the music changed to the haunting melody that was her cue. She took a deep breath, then walked from behind the curtain and made her way slowly along the catwalk, hearing the faint but appreciative gasp from the audience as behind her enlargements of that hauntingly beautiful photograph slid silently down into place. She hadn't been keen when Denis had explained that they intended to use the photo as a backdrop, but she had to admit that it had been a clever move. The audience appeared transfixed as one after the other the pictures slid into place.

Reaching the end of the walkway, Maggie paused and made a slow half-turn, as she'd been instructed to do, seeming to hesitate when she saw the life-sized images blocking her way back. She held the pose for a moment then turned to make her way down the steps and out through the doors at the back of the room, doing her best to appear as wistful as she had in the photograph.

Her eyes met those of the man who was sitting right beside the steps, and she felt shock spear through her so sharply that she stumbled, her face going ashen. He came to his feet at once, reaching out to steady her, but his fingers barely had time to brush her arm before she recovered and fled past him from the room. Behind her she heard a stunned silence followed by a huge round of applause, then the doors swung to and cut off the sound.

'Are you all right?'

She hadn't realised that he had been quick enough to follow her out, and now she spun round, the stiff, shimmering folds of the black silk-taffeta rustling as they fell and swirled around her legs.

'Damn you, Matthew, how dare you do this to me? How dare you follow me here tonight?' There was a raw pain in her voice and in the depths of her eyes as she faced him across the brightly lit foyer. 'Do you get some sort of perverted kick from pursuing me this way?'

One dark brow quirked upwards but his tone was surprisingly mild when he answered her. 'I didn't follow you, Maggie. It's pure coincidence that we are both here. Don't be so quick to jump to conclusions.'

'You weren't following me? Then what are you doing here?' There was a scornful disbelief in her voice as she laughed, feeling the pain dissolving into a huge wave of anger. 'Don't tell me that you have suddenly discovered an interest in *haute couture* fashion?'

'Mother is one of the organisers of this event. It's for a charity which she is particularly involved with. Normally Father would have escorted her here tonight, but...' He shrugged, his broad shoulders moving dismissively under the dark cloth of his tailored dinner jacket. The formal clothes suited him, the severe lines only serving to emphasise the splendour of his wide-shouldered, narrow-hipped physique, and Maggie looked away, hating herself for the way her heart beat a little faster at the sight of him.

'If you're worried about what the audience thought when you fled like that then don't be. I rather gather they thought it was all part of the show.'

There was a dry humour in his voice, but Maggie couldn't enjoy the joke, not when it was so close to the truth. The shock of seeing him like that had brought home to her exactly what she had been thinking about when that haunting photo had been taken: Matthew! Thoughts of him had filled her head all the time that Denis had been taking the photographs, so it was little wonder that it had been captured on film.

Matthew haunted her day and night, no matter how she tried to tell herself he didn't. Maybe he had been right and they should exorcise this passion which held them once and for all.

The thought shocked her so much that she gasped and heard him murmur in concern. He took a step towards her, but she backed away at once and his face tightened into grim lines.

'For heaven's sake, Maggie, stop that! Stop looking at me that way. Can't we even make a pretence of acting civilised for a couple of hours, seeing as fate has brought us both here?'

He was right, of course. She had to stay calm. She couldn't afford to let him get an inkling of what she'd been thinking.

'All right. Why not? We're both adults, after all.'

'Good. Now I think I had better get back inside. I shall see you later probably.'

There was cool dismissal in the way he turned his back on her to go back inside, and for some silly reason it rankled, although she wouldn't have wanted to delve too deeply into the reasons why.

'Oh, Maggie.'

The sound of her name brought her troubled eyes up to his, and she felt heat spill in slow, heavy waves along her veins when she saw how he was looking at her. In a look that seemed to scorch he let his eyes linger on the bare smoothness of her shoulders above the strapless bodice of the gown before they drifted down the length of her to where the black satin slippers peeped out from beneath the hem of the taffeta skirt. Slowly he looked back at her face, and Maggie felt an emotion so intense that it hurt her as he said quietly, 'I don't think I have ever seen you looking as beautiful as you do tonight.'

'I...' Her voice dried up, the protest lying unspoken on her lips as they stared at each other for a moment that was eternity, then Matthew walked back into the room and the doors swung shut.

Maggie shuddered, wrapping her arms around herself, but it was impossible to hold back the tide of passion now that it had risen again.

The meal was delicious, but to Maggie each mouthful might have been sawdust. Setting down her knife and fork, she picked up her glass and took a long drink of the fine wine. She never usually drank more than half a glass, but tonight was an exception. Tonight she needed the bolster it gave to her flagging courage.

Unbidden, her eyes moved across the room to Matthew's table, and she felt her heart leap when she saw that he was watching her. It had happened all night long: she would look up, to find him watching her across the room, and now her nerves were raw. It was only a reluctance to cause another scene that stopped her from getting up and leaving now, in the middle of the meal, but once it was over then she would go as fast as her legs would carry her.

However, her plans were thwarted when after the meal several people stopped by her table to compliment her on the way the photographs had been used to such startling effect. It would have been rude to walk away right then, so she stayed where she was so that the tables had been cleared and the band was playing before she was finally free to make her escape.

Smiling round at the rest of the party, she started to make her excuses, then fell silent when she spotted Matthew making his way across the room towards her, hating the hot rush of pleasure she felt as she watched him coming closer.

'Dance with me, Maggie?'

He held his hand out but she hesitated, suddenly afraid where it could lead to, before becoming aware of the interested glances from the rest of the group who were watching them. Colour stole across her cheeks and she stood up, her whole body tensing when she felt his hand slide round her waist as he guided her on to the floor and took her in his arms.

He looked down into her face, smiling infuriatingly when he saw the angry flush on her cheeks and the mutinous curve of her mouth. 'You'll turn the wine sour if you glower like that, my sweet.'

She glared up at him, holding herself rigid when he tried to ease her closer into his arms. 'Don't "my sweet" me, Matthew Kane! What do you think you're playing at? People are watching us! Do you want to start all the gossip again?'

'Let them talk if they want to.' He glanced round, with cool arrogance written all over his face. 'They would talk even more if I pretended to ignore you after what happened before.'

'Ohhh, I see. Is that why you asked me to dance, then . . . to allay any further gossip?'

'No. I asked you because I couldn't think of anything I wanted to do more than hold you in my arms and dance with you right at this moment.'

Maggie gasped in surprise, and Matthew took advantage of the moment to draw her closer into his arms, his hand running tantalisingly up from her waist to where the dress dipped low at the back, and she shuddered as she felt his fingers stroking her bare skin.

'Don't do that,' she whispered huskily.

'Do what? This?' His fingertips traced a gentle pattern across her back before he let his whole palm rest warmly against it.

'Matthew!' Why didn't she sound more indignant and less breathless? Why didn't she demand that he stop these tantalising caresses right now before they got out of hand?

'Maggie.' There was laughter in the low sound of his voice as he held her a little away from him and looked deep into her eyes. 'What's the matter? Surely you can't imagine that I am planning anything . . . untoward right here in the middle of all these very highly respected members of the community?'

'I don't know what you are planning, but whatever it is, stop it!'

'I'm not planning anything, Maggie, apart from dancing as many dances with you as you'll let me. You have my word that tonight I shall be on my best behaviour. So let's call a truce, shall we?'

It was a tantalising idea, made even more so when he took her silence for agreement and drew her closer, so that she could feel the hardness of his thighs brushing against her own, feel the solid width of his chest against the curve of her breasts. Surely there could be no harm in allowing herself these few minutes to ease the ache in her heart?

The minutes drifted past, but Maggie was barely aware of time passing. One dance led to another, their steps fitting perfectly as they moved round the floor. Dancing with Matthew again like this had unleashed emotions which had been locked inside her far too long now to be denied. When the music suddenly ended and the lights came up she stared round herself like a sleepwalker awoken from a dream. People were walking from the floor, chattering tiredly as they gathered their belongings and made their way to the cloakrooms, and abruptly she pulled herself from his arms.

'I must go. I didn't realise it was so late.'

'Barely midnight, Cinderella. Why all the panic? Haven't I behaved impeccably all night long?'

'Yes, of course. But I really must go. I never intended to stay this long.'

'Then I'm glad that I changed your mind.'

There was a husky warmth in his voice and she felt her pulse leap in a response she knew he'd seen. She walked away and went back to the table to collect her bag, willing herself to stay calm.

'How are you getting home? Did you come by car?'

She shook her head, making a great show out of smoothing a tiny piece of fluff off the smooth satin bag. 'I'll be getting a taxi, but I shall have to get changed out of this dress first.' She held her hand out in a stiffly polite little gesture, which must have looked ridiculous after the way they had danced locked in each other's arms. 'Goodnight, Matthew. I appreciate the fact that you were able to put our differences aside this evening.'

He took her hand, engulfing it in his far larger one, but instead of shaking it he lifted it to his lips and turned it over to press a kiss to her wrist, where that pulse was beating like a wild thing.

'I'm glad, too, Maggie. I enjoyed this evening. Thank you.'

The words were so conventionally polite, but there was nothing conventional about the hot glitter in his blue eyes, and Maggie drew her hand away abruptly before turning and hurrying from the room. She stopped just long enough to ask the desk clerk to call her a taxi before hurrying back to the changing-room and stripping off the gown. Most of the other models had already left, so that by the time she had handed the gown into the care of the dresser she was the last to leave.

Her footsteps echoed hollowly as she made her way to the front doors to wait for the taxi, but after

a good ten minutes there was still no sign of its
arrival and she went back to the desk.

'Was there a problem about the taxi I ordered?
It hasn't arrived yet.'

The man straightened, confusion written all over
his face. 'But the gentleman said that you wouldn't
be needing it, madam.'

'Gentleman?'

'Yes ... ahhh, there he is now.'

There was relief on the elderly man's face, but it
wasn't shared by her when she turned round and
saw Matthew standing outside at the bottom of the
steps, holding his car door open for her.

'Ready, Maggie?'

Ready? She was more than ready! She erupted
down the steps like a whirlwind, fury written all
over her beautiful face. 'Don't think you are going
to get away with this! How dare you cancel my taxi
like that?'

'I thought I'd be doing you a favour.'

'Favour! Like hell are you doing me any favours,
Matthew. I—— Stop that! What are you...?
Ohhhh!'

He shut her up by the simple and highly effective
means of kissing her hard as he lifted her into his
arms and deposited her unceremoniously into the
passenger-seat. Maggie wrenched her mouth away,
rubbing the back of her hand across her burning
lips, but he took no notice as he walked calmly
round and slid in behind the wheel.

'Now look here ...' she began, but he turned and
looked at her, determination in every grim line of
his face.

'I'm taking you home, Maggie. You can kick up any amount of fuss you like, but it won't change it.'

'I might have known you wouldn't keep your promise!'

Something crossed his face, an expression so fleeting that it had gone before she had chance to understand it. 'I always keep my promises, Maggie. Always!' He started the engine, then glanced coolly round at her as he slipped the car into gear. 'You don't need to worry. I have no intention of trying anything tonight. I just wanted to know that you were home safe. I don't need another sleepless night worrying about you getting home. Heaven knows, I'm tired enough as it is.'

He pulled the car on to the driveway and Maggie sank back into the seat, studying him from under lowered lashes. He did look tired, now that she could see him in the cold, harsh light from the dashboard, lines etched deeply on either side of his mouth. But she wouldn't allow any feelings of sympathy to sway her. He had no right to take over her life like this in such a high-handed fashion...as though she still belonged to him!

The powerful car ate up the miles as they drove across the city in silence until Matthew took a cassette from the rack and slipped it into the stereo with a wry glance in her direction. 'You used to like this one. You always said that it was soothing...remember?'

She shook her head, refusing to be mollified as the first delicate strains of her favourite Debussy tape filled the car. 'I can't say that I do.'

He sighed roughly, impatiently, his hands tightening on the steering-wheel. 'Do you always have to take this attitude?'

'Why shouldn't I? It isn't nice being tricked.'

'I wasn't trying to trick you! I just wanted to know that you had got home safely!'

'How very considerate of you!' She turned away to stare out of the window, her emotions in turmoil so that she didn't know whether she wanted to shout or to cry. In the darkened glass she could see her reflection, and just behind it Matthew's profile. Every line of his face was as familiar to her as her own, etched on the glass but etched far more deeply into her heart. She closed her eyes, letting her mind paint his image inside her head, and felt pain swamp her again at the sheer futility of it all.

Matthew was a part of her and, no matter how she might rail against it, she couldn't change the fact.

'Not far to go now. Are you tired?'

There was nothing more than a gentle concern in his voice as it carried above the soft strains of the music, and Maggie drew in a slow deep breath. She could keep up the battle and refuse to answer or she could try to finish this night as it had begun. The temptation to return to their previous harmony was just too strong.

'Just a bit. I didn't have any daytime sessions, so tonight wasn't too bad.'

'And what about Janey? Have you left her with a sitter?'

It was the first time that he had ever mentioned the child without an edge to his voice, and Maggie felt something warm flood into her heart so that unknowingly her voice softened.

'She's staying the night at the child minder's house. She was really looking forward to it, although I've been suffering all sort of guilt pangs at the idea.'

'You shouldn't. You obviously take very good care of her. I envy you, Maggie. A child is a very precious gift.'

There was a note of such sadness in his voice that she closed her eyes in despair. How could she continue denying him his child like this? What right did she have to use the pain she'd felt at his cruel rejection as an excuse? He had been so different tonight, gentler, calmer, far more approachable. Surely this would be the ideal time to tell him and maybe work things out? She wasn't fool enough to think that he would forgive her for what she'd done, but that didn't matter when she would be giving both Matthew and Janey something so very precious... each other.

'Matthew, there is something I think you should—— Look out!'

The car came out of a side-road, headlights blazing as it cut straight in front of them. Matthew swore, wrenching on the steering-wheel as he fought desperately to avoid the collision, but he didn't have a chance. There was a sickening noise of tearing metal which seemed to go on and on forever, then everything slid into slow motion as the car spun round and round before coming to rest with its bonnet buried in a garden wall.

Maggie shook her head, trying to rid herself of the sickening sound so that she could think what to do. She was shaking so hard, her heart pounding the blood along her veins, that it was a few seconds before she became aware of the absolute silence in the car, and she swung round, staring at Matthew, who was lying slumped over the wheel, a thin trickle of blood running down his cheek.

'Matthew! Matthew, are you all right? Answer me, Matthew!'

She screamed his name, her voice shrill with fear, but he just lay there, making no attempt to answer her, and she felt her heart contract. Please, please, let him be all right!

The tea was far too sweet, making her stomach churn as she forced herself to drink it rather than offend the young policeman who had insisted on making it for her. Setting the cup back down, she stared across the room at the brown-painted door.

What was going on in there? Matthew had been closeted with the police inspector for well over half an hour now, ever since the doctor had left after checking the bump on his head and issuing a stern warning to go straight to hospital if he experienced any headache or double vision. Maggie had wanted him to go when the ambulance had arrived at the scene of the accident, but he had refused, over-riding her protests. He had been almost curt as he had brushed her aside to speak to the police officers attending the accident, and she had felt ridiculously hurt, and inexplicably worried.

Even allowing for the fact that he must be furious that the other car had just driven off after causing the accident, Maggie had sensed that there was something else bothering him, a feeling heightened by the speed with which they had been taken to the nearest police station. What was going on?

The door opened and she jumped to her feet as Matthew came out. She hurried across the room, studying his face with anxious eyes, but apart from a livid bruise on his temple he looked little the worse for his ordeal.

He paused in the doorway to shake the inspector's hand then turned, his eyes sliding quickly over her worried face before he drew her close and held her for a moment.

'You OK?'

Maggie nodded, clinging hold of him, remembering her fear when she had looked round and seen him lying slumped against the wheel. She never wanted to go through a repeat of that!

'Right, let's get out of here, shall we?' His voice was brusque as he slid an arm round her shoulders and steered her from the building, and Maggie shot him a curious look, sensing the tension in him.

'Are you all right?'

'Yes, or at least I will be once I get out of here.'

He said no more, his expression so grim that she fell silent and let him lead her out to the courtyard, where a car was waiting, evidently to take them home.

As he saw the surprise on her face his expression softened for a moment. 'A bit of royal treatment for us, eh? The inspector offered to have a car run us home, so I saw no reason to refuse.'

'Of course not. I just didn't expect it, that's all.'

She slid into the back seat, leaving Matthew to climb in next to the driver, and sat silently as they drove through the quiet streets. It was already four in the morning, but she had hardly noticed the time passing since they had first set out on the journey home, yet she couldn't rid herself of the feeling that there was something going on that she didn't know about.

The car dropped them off outside her house. Maggie unlocked the door, stepping wearily into the hall to switch on the light. In the bright glare her hair flamed with a red fire as it fell around her shoulders, and she heard Matthew draw in a sharp, fierce breath as he reached out and pulled her almost roughly into his arms.

'I would never forgive myself if anything happened to you because of me, Maggie!'

There was anguish in his deep voice and she drew back to stare into his face in concern. 'It wasn't your fault, Matthew. That car came out of nowhere. Nobody could have avoided the crash.' She smoothed her hands up and down his back, feeling the tension in the rigid muscles. 'I'm all right, honestly. Not even a scratch to show for the mishap. It's just a shame that your beautiful car is a total write-off.'

'Never mind the car. It's replaceable...you aren't!' His hand slid into her hair, firm and strong as he caught the back of her head and drew her to him while he kissed her mouth with a lingering tenderness. 'I shall never forgive myself for letting you get involved in this.'

'In what? What is going on, Matthew? What aren't you telling me?' She tried to move away, wanting to make him explain, but he wouldn't let her go and after a moment she stopped struggling. Maybe there was something going on that he wasn't telling her about, but for now it was enough to be in his arms, feel his warmth, his strength, to know that he was alive.

They stayed like that for several minutes, just holding each other, then slowly Matthew put her from him, stepping back to run a hand over his dishevelled hair and down the front of his white shirt, which was spotted with blood now from the cut on his temple.

'I'm a mess. I think I'd better ring for a taxi and get on home and let you get into bed for what is left of the night.'

There was a rent in the shoulder seam of his dinner-jacket and more dried blood encrusted on the satin lapels, and Maggie reached out to run a trembling finger across the patches. 'You gave me a terrible fright before. I...I thought...' She tailed off, unable to put those horribly vivid fears into words, and heard him swear softly under his breath. He caught her by the arms, holding her firmly in front of him as he stared into her eyes. 'It's all over now, Maggie. You must try and put it right out of your mind. It was just a horrible accident. You'll feel better after a night's sleep.'

She forced a shaky smile to her lips. 'I probably shall. Do you want a drink, coffee or something, before you go?'

He shook his head, a wry smile on his mouth as he let her go. 'I could do with a stiff drink but I'm under strict orders from the doctor not to have one, so I shall have to obey him.'

'You should have gone to the hospital. Head injuries are dangerous. You never know if you might take a turn for the worse later on.'

'I'll be fine. Don't worry about me.'

'But I am worried.' She drew in a tiny little breath, knowing that she would never rest at the thought of his going home to an empty house and possibly being taken ill. 'I want you to stay here tonight, Matthew. Just so that I can keep an eye on you.'

'I don't think that would be a good idea.'

'Why not?' She stood up straighter, determined to have her way. 'Look, Matthew, be sensible about this. You shouldn't be on your own, just in case you need help, so logically it would be sensible to stay here.'

'Mmm, very sensible.'

There was something in his voice, a deep sensuality, that made the heat flow along her veins, and she glared at him.

'Stop that, Matthew! I know what you're trying to do, but it won't work. Now will you stay, or what?'

He shrugged, flexing his shoulders tiredly under the ruined jacket. 'Why not? I must admit that the thought of trailing back across town at this hour doesn't appeal, so yes, I will be only too glad to take you up on the offer.'

'Good. I'm glad you've decided to be sensible. I'll make a bed up for you in the sitting-room. The settee converts into a double bed, so you should be quite comfortable there.'

'I know where I would be even more comfortable, Maggie.'

The warmth in his deep voice stopped her in her tracks as she turned to hurry along the hall. She stared at him uncertainly, wondering if she had made a mistake, and saw him smile in wry self-mockery as he reached out to brush his thumb gently across the soft curve of her lips.

'I'm just teasing you, Maggie. I'm too damned tired to try to take advantage of you even if I hadn't already given you my word that I shall be on my best behaviour. So off you go and make up that bed in the sitting-room. You can sleep easy, knowing that you have my word that I will stay there and not try to join you in yours.'

She'd sleep even easier if he were lying beside her. The thought slid into her head as she hurried up the stairs to collect sheets and blankets to make up the couch, yet she made no attempt to push it aside. Tonight had shaken her, made her realise that life was far too short to waste by playing games. She loved Matthew, and in the morning she was going to take her courage in both hands and tell him that, then tell him about Janey. Having seen the new tenderness in his face, she was suddenly hopeful that they would be able to work things out.

CHAPTER EIGHT

THE tantalising aroma of fresh coffee assailed her nostrils and Maggie stirred, rolling over in the bed.

'So I was right ... coffee does still wake you up in the morning.'

There was laughter in Matthew's deep voice as he ran a finger lightly down her cheek in a gentle caress, and Maggie's eyes flew open, her heart leaping when she saw him bending over her. He had shed the ruined shirt and was wearing only the dark trousers, and she felt her senses stir at the sight of him standing there, his skin gleaming golden in the pale wintry sunlight spilling in through the window. Just for a moment she almost succumbed to the temptation to run her hands across his bare chest to feel the warmth and the hardness of the muscles under their light coating of fine black hair until deliberately she forced the desire aside.

Last night she had made up her mind to talk to Matthew today and tell him everything that needed to be said, and she must do so without any physical desire clouding the issues.

However, it seemed that Matthew had ideas of his own as he watched her sit up against the headboard. His eyes darkened and he set the cup down before sitting on the side of the bed and pulling her into his arms to kiss her with a hungry urgency that sent all common sense winging out of the window. Maggie gasped, holding herself rigid for a brief moment before suddenly relaxing in his arms and returning the kiss with a fervour that bordered on desperation. What if it all went wrong and he refused to believe that she still loved him? Surely then she would be glad of any kind of help, physical or otherwise?

He drew back slowly, cupping her cheek as he tilted her face up to his. 'Well, good morning. I would have tried that before if I'd had any idea of the kind of response I would get!'

Maggie flushed, pushing at his bare chest with her hands, but he just laughed softly and pulled her closer, trapping her hands helplessly between them. 'Don't tell me you're embarrassed? We were married, Maggie. Remember?'

Of course she remembered, and that was the whole trouble. It would have been so easy to start again without the ghost of that marriage lying between them. 'Yes, I remember. Look, Matthew, there is something I need to talk to you about; something I have to tell you.'

He frowned, letting her go as he stood up. 'There's a lot we both have to talk about, but not right now. I'll go and get a shower first, then we can talk.'

He walked from the room, leaving her staring after him in surprise at the abrupt change of his mood. It was almost as though he hadn't wanted to hear what she had to say. It didn't bode well for the future conversation, but she was still determined to get everything out in the open at last.

She got out of bed and slipped on a robe before hurrying downstairs and pouring herself another cup of coffee, sitting down at the table while she sipped it and tried to work out what she would say to him. It was going to be one of the hardest things she had ever had to do, to tell him that she still loved him and lay herself bare, but she had to do that before she told him about Janey. It was the only way she could ever make him understand.

The shower stopped running and she stood up, feeling her heart starting to hammer in anticipation of what was to come. Crossing over to the counter, she refilled the coffee-pot and started a fresh brew, then nearly jumped six feet into the air as the front doorbell rang. Glancing at the clock, she frowned as she hurried along the hall, praying that she would be able to get rid of the unwanted visitor. She couldn't face the thought of having to put off telling Matthew yet again.

'Surprise! Bet you never expected to see me so soon.' David stepped inside the hall, smiling broadly as he lifted her off her feet and swung her round in a bear-hug before setting her back down again with a puzzled frown when he saw her white face. 'Maggie? Are you all right? I didn't mean to give you a shock.'

Maggie shook her head, all too conscious of the ominous silence from upstairs. 'No, of course you didn't. Well, not exactly a shock, just a surprise. I never expected you back so soon.'

David frowned, sensing the tension yet not understanding what was causing it. 'I didn't expect to be back yet but Langton had already made up his mind about what he wanted, so there was no problem about working out the details. Look, Maggie, are you sure you're feeling OK?'

'She's fine, probably just a bit disconcerted to see you here. You always did have a lousy sense of timing, David.'

A shudder ran through Maggie as she heard Matthew, and she turned round, her face going ashen when she saw him standing at the top of the stairs. He hadn't bothered to get dressed before coming down, just wound a towel around his hips, and she felt sick at how it must seem to David to see him standing there half naked.

'Why, Maggie? Why in heaven's name after what he did to you? Dammit, have you no sense at all?' David's face was suffused with angry colour, his eyes like steel as they moved from his brother to pin her with a look filled with such pain that she put her hand out in an instinctive attempt to offer comfort, which was forestalled when Matthew came the rest of the way down the stairs and slid his arm around her shoulders.

'I would have thought the reason why was obvious, David, even to you.'

There was such harshness in Matthew's voice that Maggie flinched, pulling herself away from him, but his fingers bit into her shoulder to hold her at his side.

'Did you plan this, then, Matthew?' David asked bitterly, his eyes moving from where his brother's hand laid claim to her. 'Was this the reason why you decided to come back when you did, knowing I would be out of the country?'

Matthew shrugged. 'Let's just say that I saw my opportunity and took it. Frankly, it made no difference whether you were away or not. I could have had Maggie any time I chose!'

'Why, you bast——!'

David lunged towards him, but Maggie moved
even more swiftly and stepped between the men.
'No! Stop it, David. I won't let you fight over me!'

David swung away, pounding his fist against the
wall. 'I don't believe this! I just don't believe you
could willingly choose to go back to him after what
he did.' He turned to face her, new lines etched on
his face so that suddenly he looked far older. 'Tell
me the truth, Maggie. Was this *your* decision?'

'I...' She fell silent, pain twisting her heart when
she saw the expression in David's eyes, saw what
she had been trying to avoid seeing all this time,
that he was in love with her.

'Tell him, Maggie.'

Matthew's voice was surprisingly soft, and she
turned to look at him, seeing with a sense of grief
that he too knew how David felt about her. It was
all so fruitless: David loved her, she loved Matthew,
and Matthew...Matthew just loved playing one off
against the other for his own ends. She might never
be able to give David what he wanted but neither
would she hurt him any more by giving him false
hope.

'I asked Matthew to stay the night.'

There was a moment when she thought that
David was going to say something more, before he
turned and let himself out of the door. Maggie felt
tears fill her eyes and abruptly pulled away from
Matthew's hold, walking quickly to the kitchen to
stare blindly out of the window, feeling David's pain
as though it were her own.

'It was the kindest thing to do.'

She swung round, her hair flying, her eyes wild and glittering with unshed tears. 'Kind? To hurt someone who has never done anything but try to help you? You call that being *kind*?'

His face tightened. 'Yes, kind! You know damned well that you don't love him, so the kindest thing to do was to make the cut quick and sure.'

She laughed bitterly. 'So that's how you see it, is it? Quick and sure? Is that why you came downstairs like that, to deliberately let him think that we had been sharing the same bed last night? Did it amuse you to see the shock on his face? Did you get some sort of a kick out of watching him being hurt? Damn you, Matthew, he's your brother! Surely you have some sort of feelings left for him?'

'My brother...yes, he's that all right. He was that when he took my wife into his bed, so don't give me all that high-minded talk about feelings!' He strode across the room, magnificent in his near-naked fury as he towered over her. 'I know what it feels like to get kicked in the teeth, to have my life ripped apart!' He grasped her chin, staring into her eyes, yet she had the feeling that he wasn't really seeing her but looking backwards. 'Do you want to know how I felt when I went to David's flat that day and found you in his bed? Do you want to know that *I* felt as though the world had just caved in around me? I've been there, Maggie! I know what it feels like and, frankly, I'm glad that my *brother* has had a taste of it now!'

He flung her away from him, striding from the room and up the stairs. Maggie wanted to run after him, wanted to make him understand once and for all what really had been going on that afternoon, but in her heart she knew that it would be impossible to cut through that bitterness with mere words. The pain had grown too deep over the years, eating into him like a cancer.

She closed her eyes, remembering that dreadful day, which had started out so full of hope. She had gone to the doctor's, half suspecting that the bouts of sickness she'd been having were not the product of some virus, and had had her pregnancy confirmed. She had left the surgery, filled with joy at what it could mean. Their marriage had been shaky for several months by then and she had seen the coming baby as a chance for them to start afresh. When the bout of nausea had hit her so suddenly she had barely had time to get to David's flat, which was on her way home. He had taken one look at her pale face and put her to bed, and that was where Matthew had found her an hour or so later.

She drew in a shuddering breath, remembering what he had said, all the cruel accusations. She had tried to explain, to protest her innocence, but he had refused to listen, blinded by the jealousy that had been building inside him for months, so that in the end she had stopped trying and sat cold and remote while the bitter tirade had rained down on her head.

She couldn't have told him then about the baby, couldn't have borne to hear him say that it wasn't his, so she had guarded her secret even through the ensuing divorce, terrified by then that if he ever found out he might sue for custody. How bitterly ironic that virtually the same thing had happened yet again today.

The front door slammed and she started nervously, running along the hall to drag it open with hands that shook.

'Matthew!' She called his name but he didn't stop, and after a few minutes she went back inside and closed the door, wishing she weren't such a coward. She should have run after him and told him there and then what she should have told him three years ago, but she didn't think she could stand it any better now if he threw it all back in her face.

The events of the morning left her restless and unsettled, feelings which Janey seemed to sense once she had brought her home. After lunch she refused to go down for her nap, and in desperation Maggie dressed her in a warm quilted suit and let her play out in the back garden, digging in the sand-pit.

Pouring herself yet another cup of coffee, she leant against the counter, watching as Janey bustled to and fro, chattering to herself as she made wobbly little sandpies. It was so hard to know what to do next for the best, whether she should get in touch with Matthew and ask him to come round, or leave things as they were to cool down. She never usually felt so ambivalent about making a decision, and on the rare occasions when she had she had always rung David to ask his advice, but obviously that was out of the question now.

The telephone rang and she emptied the cooling coffee down the sink with a grimace of distaste before going to answer it. It was a wrong number, but it seemed to take a ridiculously long time to convince the caller of that fact. Finally, in exasperation, she put the receiver down and cut him off, then went back into the kitchen.

The sun was just sliding behind a cloud, leaving the small garden grey and uninviting, and she peered out of the window so that she could call Janey back inside. However, there was no sign of the child by the sand-pit now, and Maggie frowned as she hurried out of the door and looked round for her. The garden was neatly fenced on all sides so that Janey couldn't wander out into the back lane, but no matter how hard she scoured the bushes she could see no sign of her and a single cold shaft of fear raced down her spine.

She ran to the back gate, feeling the fear intensifying when it swung open at her touch. It was always kept securely locked with a sturdy bolt, which was far too difficult for a small child to draw, but somehow Janey must have managed it and got out.

She wrenched it open, shouting Janey's name as she ran along the lane and into the adjoining street, but there was no sign of her anywhere. Consumed with panic, Maggie ran back to the house and tore at the bushes, scratching her hands and face as she struggled to part them just in case Janey was playing a trick on her and hiding, but there was nothing there, nothing but the bucket and spade lying abandoned on the ground.

With a sob of fear she raced into the house, reaching for the telephone to call the police, then stopped when she saw the envelope lying on the mat. It was just an ordinary cheap brown envelope like a hundred others sent each day, yet there was

something inexplicably ominous about the way it
was lying there like that.

Her hands shook as she dropped the receiver and
snatched it up, almost ripping the thin sheet of
paper it contained in her haste.

> Tell Kane he knows what to do if he wants to
> see his child alive.

'No!' Even as she screamed the denial aloud,
Maggie knew that it was useless to try to deny the
truth. Janey could never have opened the gate by
herself, would never have wandered off after all the
warnings she'd had. Someone had taken her, and
the reason for it had something to do with Matthew!

She was shaking so much that it took three attempts to find the number for his chambers in the
phone book and ring, only to be greeted by a cool
female voice informing her that Mr Kane was
unavailable.

Maggie bit back an urge to scream at the woman,
curtly informing her that this was an emergency. It
obviously did the trick because Matthew came on
the line within seconds, his tone brusque when he
realised who was calling.

'Look, Maggie, I don't know what——'

'Janey's gone!'

The hysteria in her voice brought him up short
and he hesitated before saying quickly, 'Gone
where?'

'She's been . . . been . . .' A sob rose in her throat,
choking off the words as she sank helplessly to her
knees in front of the telephone.

'Maggie! Are you there? Maggie, for heaven's
sake . . . answer me!'

'You have to come, Matthew. Someone has taken Janey. They left a note. I don't understand it but it has something to do with you!'

'What did it say? Pull yourself together, Maggie!' The urgency in his tone was just what she needed and she drew in a shuddery breath, fighting for control. 'It says that if you want to see her alive again then you know what to do. What's going on, Matthew? Tell me!'

He ignored her plea. 'I'll be there just as fast as I can. Don't do anything until I get there. D'you understand, Maggie? You mustn't call the police or do anything at all!'

'Yes, but...'

The line went dead and slowly she replaced the receiver, praying that he knew what he was doing. The thought of some stranger having Janey was almost more than she could stand.

He must have broken all records getting across town because he was at the house within half an hour. Maggie hurried to let him in, her whole body trembling as he pulled her briefly into his arms before urging her into the sitting-room.

'Let me see the note.'

She gave it to him, watching while he read the crudely cut-out letters pasted to the cheap sheet of paper, and heard him curse with a dreadful vehemence.

'Do you know who it's from?'

Her voice was a mere thread of sound, hoarse and raspy from the fear that was lodged in her throat, and a spasm of pain crossed his face. 'Yes. The same people who staged that little accident last night.'

'Staged the... You mean that somebody deliberately did that?'

'Yes.' He ran a hand over his face, which was grey under the tan, his lips rimmed with a white line that told of the strain he was feeling. 'There have been a number of similar incidents since the trial first began, but I never suspected that they would go this far to force my hand.'

'You mean this all has to do with the bullion trial... that accident, and now Janey?'

'Yes.'

'But why didn't you tell me, warn me? I would never have let her out of my sight if I'd had an inkling of what was going on. Damn you, Matthew, why didn't you tell me?' Hysteria turned to fury and found an outlet as she hurled the accusations at him, so caught up in her own anguish that she never saw the agony on his face.

'I didn't tell you because I never thought they would involve you in any way. Yes, there have been other things going on, but this...' he tapped the paper '...this is in a league of its own. Obviously they must have seen us together and know who you are, so they've added two and two and decided that's where Janey fits in. They are using her as a lever to make me agree to their demands, but once they know they've got it wrong they'll have to let her go.'

Maggie shook her head, sickness spilling into her stomach. 'No, they won't. They haven't got anything wrong.'

He frowned, standing up to pace the floor as though he found it impossible to sit still. 'Of course they have. They think she's my daughter, and that's the only reason they've taken her. Once I let it be known that they're wrong then I can guarantee that they'll give her back. Believe me, Maggie, these men know what they're doing and they won't risk a life sentence for kidnapping.'

Maggie stood up, her legs shaking as she walked to the bureau and drew a small piece of paper from a folder and held it out to him. 'They haven't made any mistakes. Janey is your daughter.'

He took the birth certificate, staring down at it for long seconds before raising his eyes to her face, and Maggie shrank back from the fury etched on his face.

'Damn you, Magdalena, damn you to hell for keeping this from me!'

He tossed the certificate aside and strode out of the room. Maggie ran after him, catching hold of his arm as he wrenched the door open.

'Where are you going? Matthew! What are you going to do?'

He shook her off, sending her reeling against the wall with the force of the action. 'To get my daughter back!'

'Matthew, I——'

'Don't!' he snarled. 'If you have any sense at all then don't say a word apart from praying that your selfish stupidity won't cost you our child!'

'You know where she is?'

'I think I do...hope I do. Let's just pray that I'm right.'

'Be...be careful, Matthew.' There was a broken note in her voice and he turned to stare at her, his eyes cold as ice as they swept over her white face in a look that burned with dislike.

'I shall take care all right, of me and my daughter, and do you want to know why, my sweet? Do you?' He leaned closer, pinning her with a stare that cut through to her heart. 'Because once I get *my* daughter back then I am going to make it my business to see that you pay for what you've done!'

He left without another word, but it was a long time before she found the strength to close the door.

CHAPTER NINE

TIME passed so slowly. Maggie paced the floor until sheer exhaustion forced her to sit down, but she couldn't rest. Matthew had sounded so certain that he would be able to get Janey back, but what if he had made a mistake and he couldn't find her? As the hours passed, Maggie became less sure that she had done the right thing in agreeing to his demands that she shouldn't call the police.

Finally, at a little after midnight, when she could stand the waiting no longer, she went to the phone to make the call, praying that she hadn't left it too late. The sound of a car door slamming and footsteps coming quickly up the path made her drop the receiver, and she ran to the door and flung it open, her heart surging in relief when she saw Matthew coming up the path carrying a sleeping Janey in his arms.

With a broken sob she ran out to meet them, lifting the child from him to hold her close as she buried her face in the soft dark curls.

'Thank you ... thank you,' she whispered brokenly, looking up at him with tears streaming unchecked down her face.

He ignored her thanks, taking her by the arm to usher her brusquely back inside the house, his face like a mask. 'She needs to be put to bed. I don't think she's hurt in any way, but obviously she must be confused about what has happened. I told her that it had been a little game and maybe she will believe that. We shall have to see.'

He walked away into the sitting-room and poured himself a drink, downing it in one go before standing with head bowed as he stared at the empty glass.

Maggie watched him for a moment, then turned to carry Janey up the stairs to bed, feeling her heart aching. He had done what he had said he would, got Janey back, but it wouldn't end here. This was just the beginning, and she was suddenly terrified of what was to follow. She only had to remember his face when he had found out that Janey was his child to know that he would never forgive her now, and maybe he was right. Unwittingly she had risked Janey's life by her deliberate attempt to keep him from finding out the truth.

It took only minutes to undress the child and tuck her up in bed, but Maggie lingered, stroking the soft dark hair back from the flushed little cheeks, wanting just to reassure herself that Janey was all right.

'How is she?'

She jumped when Matthew came quietly into the room, cradling a full glass as he came over to the bed and stared down at the child. Maggie moved away, making a great show out of smoothing the covers, something about the expression on his face making her deeply uneasy.

'She's fine, just worn out by it all. Where did you find her, Matthew? Who had her?'

He flicked her a hard glance, taking a long swallow of the drink before he answered with a deliberate curtness. 'That is none of your business.

Now if you have finished up here I suggest you come downstairs. It's time you and I had a talk.'

There was a barely restrained anger in his voice, and Maggie felt her stomach lurch. She led the way back downstairs, sitting down on a chair with her hands clasped in her lap, watching as Matthew walked straight across the room and topped up his drink.

'Do you think it's wise to drink like that? You've had two already, one on top of the other.'

'Probably not, but at least while I'm holding this glass I'm keeping my hands off you!' He smiled unpleasantly, his eyes glacial as he took a long deliberate swallow. 'It would afford me great pleasure to wring your pretty little neck, Maggie, dearest, for what you've done to me and that child upstairs, but that would be far too easy a let-out for you, so I shall restrain myself. You deserve to suffer, and I shall take great pleasure in seeing that you do!'

'Stop it!' She came to her feet in a rush, her face paper-white, her whole body trembling at the note of sheer hatred in his voice. 'Look, Matthew, I know you're upset, but once you have time to think things through then you'll see that talk like that will serve no purpose whatsoever. We have to be sensible about all this, try to work things out for Janey's sake!'

'Work things out? Damn you, Maggie, you tell me how we can work out your lying and cheating? You tell me how we can "work out" the fact that you quite deliberately deceived me and denied me knowledge of my own child?' He flung the glass across the room so that it shattered against the wall, and she shrank back, but he caught her by the arms, shaking her until her head rolled from side to side. 'I knew you hated me, Maggie, I just didn't know how much!'

'No!' Fear and a strange inexplicable need to erase the anguish she could see on his face warred inside her, and fear lost. She grasped his hands, holding them tightly with her own as she willed him to hear the truth and understand. 'I didn't do it because I hated you. I did it because I was afraid!'

'Afraid?' He stared at her in disbelief for a moment, then let her go so abruptly that she staggered. Running a hand over his hair, he dropped down into one of the chairs, his face suddenly grey. 'I never laid a finger on you, Maggie, so how can you claim to have been afraid of me?'

'Not physically.' She swallowed hard, feeling the tension humming along her limbs from the sheer effort it cost to hold on to her control. 'I was afraid that you wouldn't believe the child I was carrying was yours! Be honest, Matthew, remember how many times you accused me of having affairs with different men, even your own brother. When I found out that I was pregnant I was over the moon; I couldn't wait to tell you, but then you found me at David's flat and all the accusations started again. I couldn't bear the thought that you might deny the child was yours, and equally I couldn't bear the thought that if you did believe it you might try and take it from me.' She smiled bitterly. 'Lord knows that our marriage was shaky at the best of times. I used to wonder why you had married me until I came to the conclusion that it was because you couldn't have me any other way!' Her eyes met his, cloudy with memories. 'I was so innocent when we met, you see. If I had been more sophisticated then maybe none of this would ever have happened and we wouldn't be trying to tear each other apart. We would have had an affair, maybe lived together until you tired of me, but never marriage. I never fitted into your lifestyle and I knew it, right from the beginning.'

He shook his head. 'That's just an excuse. It wasn't a question of your fitting in. All you needed to do was love me, Maggie, but you weren't capable of that!'

'I did!' And I still do, she added silently, but there was no way she could say that now. They had gone way beyond that point in the past few hours. Now all she could hope for was to convince him not to try to carry out his threat to make her suffer for the way she had hurt him, but she knew the moment he spoke again that that would be an impossible task.

'You have no idea of what love means! It's all a game to you, Maggie. You like attention, enjoy being the very centre of adulation. A husband wasn't enough for you. You wanted more, from any man who crossed your path! Our marriage could have worked if you'd let it!'

'It wasn't all my fault! It takes two to make a marriage work, but how typical that you should blame me rather than admit to your own failings! I loved you, Matthew, and I wanted our marriage to work, but it was your insane jealousy that tore us apart! You wanted to own me, body and soul, but no one can do that to another person...not even you!'

'You think not?' He stood up, towering over her, although he made no attempt to touch her. 'Then you are going to find out very quickly how wrong you are, my sweet.'

'I don't know what you mean.' She turned away, cold shivers running through her at the expression on his face. He caught her wrist, his fingers surprisingly gentle, yet Maggie knew that it would be impossible to break free without a struggle, and something inside her shied away from doing that.

'It's quite simple, Maggie. I am going to own you!'

'I ... don't be ridiculous!' She tried to inject mockery into her voice, but she could tell that it hadn't been successful when he smiled with that hard assurance she hated so much.

'Not ridiculous, my love, just plain, hard fact. Until I finally become tired of you then I shall own you, body and soul, as you so picturesquely put it. And do you want to know why you will agree?'

She shook her head. 'No. I don't want to hear anything you have to say. You're crazy if you think you can coerce me into doing something I don't want to do. I'm not some young gullible girl now, Matthew. I'm a grown woman, and there's nothing you can threaten me with that will make me fall in with your crazy plans!'

'Nothing? Not even the promise that I will take Janey away from you if you fight me?' He smiled cruelly, watching the shock settle on her face.

'You can't! There isn't a court in the land that will let you do that!'

'Isn't there? You forget that I have a very good idea of what courts can and can't do, and giving custody to a father is becoming increasingly commonplace nowadays. But, of course, if you are prepared to gamble then be my guest.' He let her go, walking from the room, leaving her staring after him until she came to her senses.

'Wait!' She ran after him into the hall, blocking his way as he went to open the front door. 'You can't just walk away after threatening me like that. I want to know what you intend to do. Damn it, Matthew, I'm her mother!'

'And I'm her father, so that gives me rights as well. It's just a pity that you have managed to overlook that fact all these years, isn't it?'

There was a bitter anger in his voice as he reached past her to unlock the door, and Maggie felt tears fill her eyes as she realised what was behind it. How would she have felt if the situation had been reversed, and she had been the one kept out of Janey's life?

'I'm sorry, Matthew. I know what I did was wrong, but can't you at least try and understand why I did it?'

He shook his head, his hand clenching into a fist as it rested against the lock. 'No, I damned well can't. I don't care what you say, Maggie, but nothing...*nothing* gave you the right to do what you did! Now, unless you are intending to fall in with my plans even sooner than I anticipated, I suggest that you step aside and let me leave.'

Maggie moved away from the door, her head bowed so that he couldn't see the anguish on her face. She could well understand his anger, but it didn't help her situation now. What was she going to do?

He opened the door then stopped, staring down at her bent head. 'I'm not an unreasonable man, Maggie. I shall give you forty-eight hours to get your things sorted out.'

She frowned, glancing quickly up at him. 'What things? I don't understand.'

He smiled, his eyes glittering with a harsh intensity. 'Clothes, toys for Janey, et cetera, et cetera. What were you expecting, that I would visit you here? I'm afraid that isn't my idea at all. You and Janey are moving in with me, and I shall give you forty-eight hours to get your things together.'

'No! I won't do it... I won't!' There was desperation that bordered on hysteria in her voice, but he just smiled, reaching out to slide his hand round the back of her neck as he pulled her to him and took her mouth in a kiss that was more of an insult than a caress.

He let her go, lifting a long strand of her hair from where it clung to his collar to smooth it back behind her ear. 'Oh, you will, Maggie... you will, once you've had time to think what the alternative could be.'

His footsteps echoed as he walked down the path. Maggie closed the door abruptly, leaning back against it as her legs started to buckle, feeling the sickness of panic welling up inside her.

She had to do something to stop this now, but what? What could she do to stop Matthew from carrying out this new, dreadful threat?

The next couple of days passed in a daze of despair and confusion as she tried to find a solution. Several times she toyed with the idea of just taking Janey

and running away, far away, where Matthew
wouldn't find them, but each time common sense
reasserted itself. Her home, her work, everything
was here in London, and there was no way she could
just up and leave. Although she had some money
in the bank, it wouldn't last long, not with the demands of a growing child to support. She couldn't
throw away everything she had fought so hard for,
nor could she just toss aside all the stability she had
always tried to give to Janey's life.

Fortunately the child had apparently accepted
that the kidnapping had been some sort of a game,
and Maggie had tried to foster this idea. However,
there was no knowing what effect another sudden
upheaval could have on a young and vulnerable
child. Somehow there must be a way to convince
Matthew that what he planned was wrong in the
extreme, but as the deadline drew nearer and nearer
she was still no closer to finding the answer.

Desperate to keep herself occupied rather than
give in to the debilitating despair that was growing
ever stronger, she accepted a last-minute assignment for a photographic session. It might have
been the coward's way out, but while she was away
from the house then at least Matthew couldn't come
and find her. Even another few hours were welcome
breathing-space as she tried to make plans.

She took extra care with her make-up for the
session, knowing that the sleepless nights had taken
their toll, and was just putting the finishing touches
to her face when the changing-room door opened
and Marie walked in.

'Well, hello, stranger,' she said, putting the lip-
brush down and turning to smile at her friend.

'Where have you been? Somewhere lovely and hot, from the look of that gorgeous tan.'

Marie smiled, tossing her bag on to the floor before dropping into a chair. 'Jamaica.'

'Jamaica! Good heavens. What made you go there?' Maggie stared at the other woman in concern, noticing the strain under the tan, the faint shadows under her huge dark eyes.

'I had an offer I couldn't refuse.' Marie sat up and started to unpin her hair, staring defiantly at her through the mirror. 'You remember Paul Anderson, don't you?'

'The photographer we worked with a couple of months back? Yes, of course I do, but I never realised that you two were so...so friendly.'

'I doubt if we are now.' Marie shook her hair back from her face, wry humour in her expression. 'I'm afraid Paul and I didn't part on the best of terms.'

'And could that have had anything to do with Denis? He's been like a bear with a sore head since you went off. What are you playing at, Marie? If you're trying to make him jealous then just be careful that you don't push him too far.'

'I know. It was a crazy thing to do, but at the time I just couldn't take any more. I decided it was time to cut my losses and find someone else.' She laughed bitterly. 'That was a joke. Poor Paul, it's no wonder he wasn't amused when he discovered that the woman he had invited on holiday could think of no one but another man! Still, enough of my problems, Mags. You seem to have enough of your own right now. I read about Matthew in the paper this morning when I was on my way here. I

must say that I found it hard to believe. He didn't
strike me as a man who would do that sort of a
thing.'

'What do you mean? Why was Matthew in the
paper?' There was a sharp anxiety in her voice, and
Marie turned to her in surprise.

'Haven't you seen it? Here, I've still got my copy.
Take a look for yourself.'

Maggie took the paper, flicking through the
pages, then felt her heart stop when she saw
Matthew's picture on one of them. Just for a
moment the print blurred as the blood rushed to
her head before determinedly she forced herself to
read the few brief paragraphs with a total disbelief.

It must be a mistake, a horrible, dreadful
mistake! Why else should the paper claim that
Matthew had been dismissed from the bullion
robbery trial and was now facing possible charges
of perverting the course of justice?

'Didn't you know?'

She shook her head, unable to speak as she read
and re-read the report.

'It seems strange to me. Oh, I know I only met
him that once at your house that night, but I would
have sworn on a stack of bibles that he was as
straight as a die. There must have been a really good
reason why he would have done such a thing, don't
you think, Maggie?'

The thought came out of nowhere, seemingly
plucked from the air, growing stronger and stronger
with every second until she felt nearly over-
whelmed by it. Suddenly she *knew* why he had done
it and her heart lifted in joy, although until she had
seen him and spoken to him she had no way of

proving it. She might be making the biggest mistake of her life, of course, but she owed it to them all, and especially to Matthew, to find out if she was right.

The street was quiet. Maggie parked the car, taking a deep breath before climbing out and walking up the steep flight of steps to the door. Her hand was shaking so hard as she pressed the bell, and she let it drop to her side, clenching her fist so that the nails bit into the palm. She had almost faltered on her way here, wondering if she was being a fool to come, but now that she was here she would see it through.

She pressed the bell again, longer, harder, determination on her face, then jumped nervously when the door was flung open.

'I have nothing else to say! Now get—— What do you want?'

There was little welcome in Matthew's tone or in the hard look from those blue eyes, but Maggie stood her ground, her heart contracting when she saw the lines of strain etched on his face.

'Hello, Matthew. How are you?'

'How do you think I am? What do you want, Maggie? Come to gloat, have you, my sweet?' He raised the glass he was holding to his lips and took a long swallow of the whiskey before looking back at her with a biting contempt that cut her to the quick. 'You must have had a field-day, reading all about it in the paper. Is that why you've come...to see the rest of the show? Well, I hate to disappoint you, but the show's over for the day.'

He started to close the door but Maggie stepped forward, taking him by surprise as she pushed her way into the hall. He obviously hadn't bothered to shave that day and his jaw was dark with beard, giving him a dangerous look that made her heart beat nervously, but there was no way he was getting rid of her until she was prepared to leave.

'I didn't come for any show, Matthew,' she said coolly, 'although from the look of it you seem to have been putting one on.' She let her eyes drift down over the rumpled folds of white shirt which was partly unbuttoned over his chest, before coming back to his face with a deliberate flicker of distaste.

'Now look here——'

'No, thank you. I don't think I want to look right now, Matthew. You really should cut back on the drinking if that's the state it leaves you in.'

His eyes flared with anger and he stepped forward, but she side-stepped him, walking quickly down the hall into the study, feeling her heart beating wildly. He followed her into the room, slamming the glass down on a table with a noisy clatter, which made her flinch inwardly but outwardly she showed no sign.

'Does that meet with your approval? Now, why have you come?'

'To see you and find out what's been going on.' She sat down in one of the huge red leather armchairs, crossing her legs, seeing the way his eyes followed the movement with a light in their depths which he wasn't quick enough to hide. And that betraying little flicker gave her hope. Suddenly she knew that she had been right to come.

She sat back in the chair, staring up at him from under her lashes, watching the hot rim of colour sweep along his cheekbones in a sudden tide. He

turned away, picking up the glass again before
setting it back down and walking across the room
to stand by the window and stare out. There was a
leashed tension in his big body which tore at her
heart, but she made herself remain seated in the
chair, although every instinct was telling her to go
to him, to put aside their differences and give him
comfort from what he was so obviously suffering.
If they were ever to work out this mess they had
made of their lives then they had to start now, no
matter how painful it would be.

'You must have seen the papers, so I don't really
know what else you want to hear. If you have come
to rub salt in the wounds, Maggie, then I'm sorry,
but you're out of luck. There have been several
dozen others here before you.' His voice was harsh,
as harsh as his expression as he turned to glare at
her across the room, but she met the look levelly.

'Yes, I've read what was in the papers. Now I
want to know why you did what you are supposed
to have done.'

'Why? That's the sixty-four thousand dollar
question, isn't it? The one on everybody's lips! Just
tell us why you did it, Mr Kane. Was it for financial
gain?' He laughed bitterly, running a hand over his
dishevelled hair and around the back of his neck
to knead the tense muscles. 'How about you telling
me why you think I did it?'

'For Janey.' She smiled when she saw the shock
in his eyes, her face very soft. 'You gave away that
evidence not for any financial incentives but for the
one thing...the only thing that would ever have
induced you to break that code of ethics you live
by...your child!'

There was silence in the room, so much silence, and she held her breath as she prayed that her shock tactics would work. If Matthew refused to admit that she was right then she was going to have her work cut out. But, no matter how hard it was, she was going to see that he didn't suffer any more because of their child.

'How did you work that out?'

He was far too good a lawyer to give anything away by his tone, but Maggie knew that what she'd suspected had been correct and her heart lifted with sudden crazy joy.

'I know you, Matthew. I know that nothing on earth would have induced you to do such a thing unless it was a matter of life or death, and that's what it was. The people who took Janey that day were after one thing from you. You knew it immediately. That's why you were so sure that you could get her back. You gave them what they wanted in exchange for her. Aren't I right?'

'Yes!' Agony crossed his face and he turned to slam his fist against the wall in a gesture of defeat. 'I knew what they wanted all right. They had tried to get it before, some papers implicating the rest of the group who had masterminded the robbery. But it was I who finally gave them away!'

'You can't blame yourself. Think what they could have done to Janey.'

'Of course I thought about it! Damn it, Maggie, they would have killed her if I hadn't given them what they wanted!'

'Then why haven't you told all this to the police?' She stood up, crossing the room to stand in front of him. 'I read all the reports in the papers, every single word, yet not once was there a mention of mitigating circumstances, a hint that there could have been a very good reason why you did such a thing. Why didn't you tell them?'

'That is none of your damned business!'

'Isn't it?' She stared up into his face with a quiet determination. 'Would you like to know what I think, Matthew?'

He shrugged, looking away from her, his face strangely tense. 'You seem to be the one with all the answers.'

'I think you told no one the truth because you didn't want us dragged into it. You were protecting Janey from all the publicity, maybe even protecting me.' She laid her hand on his arm, feeling the rigidity of the muscles under her fingers. 'Am I right?'

He froze under her touch, his eyes searching hers before abruptly he moved away and flung himself down in one of the chairs. 'Yes! There was no way I was going to let the press have a field-day by dragging our private life into the papers. Janey would have been marked for life. And it wouldn't have taken long for one of those reporters to have dug up the interesting fact that I hadn't *known* that I had a child before that day! Imagine how she would feel in years to come to learn that her mother had hated her father so much that she had even kept the fact that he had a child from him!'

His pain hurt her and she drew herself up. 'I never hated you, Matthew.'

'No? Forgive me if I find that hard to believe. Still, no matter. You have achieved what you wanted all along, Maggie.'

'What do you mean?'

'Got me out of your life once and for all.' He smiled bitterly. 'I thought I could find some peace for myself by taking my revenge on you, but what I hadn't bargained for was the fact that you are such a worthy opponent. You have turned the tables very neatly on me, my sweet. Well done!'

'Does that mean that you've given up that crazy idea of forcing me to go back with you?' Her heart was beating so hard and fast that she felt sick, filling her with a wild sweet excitement she'd tasted only briefly before in her life.

'Yes. Do you want it in black and white?'

She ignored his sarcasm, seeing through the brittle layers to what lay beneath as she should have seen through it before, but fear had blinded her to the truth.

'Good. That changes everything.' She stood up, smoothing down the skirt of the charcoal-grey suit with hands that were rock-steady now as she prepared herself to utter words she would never have imagined to hear coming from her lips just two short days before. 'In that case, then, Matthew, I suggest you start that clock again.'

'Start the . . . what are you talking about? Look, if this is some kind of a new little game to taunt me . . .'

She walked over to his chair and bent to press the tip of a finger against his lips as she smiled into his startled face. 'It's no game. Last time you were in my house you gave me forty-eight hours to get my belongings together before you came for me. So start the clock again and I shall expect you.'

'Maggie!' He tried to rise from the chair but she pushed him gently back down before walking across the room to the door. 'I don't want your pity, Maggie!'

Three years of pain lay in the harsh statement, and she turned back to face him, letting him see now in her face what she had kept hidden from him for so long.

'That's good, because pity is the last thing you will ever get from me, Matthew Kane.'

The dawning comprehension on his face almost stopped her from walking out; almost, but not quite. When ... *if* Matthew came for her then she had to be sure that he understood just what it meant. This time there could be no going back.

CHAPTER TEN

MATTHEW didn't come.

Maggie ticked another day off on the calendar, feeling another crack forming in her already broken heart. She had been so sure that she'd been right in her assessment of the situation, so sure that Matthew really did feel something for her apart from that bitter desire for revenge, but it had been nearly a week now and still she had heard nothing from him.

Tossing the pencil aside, she hurried along the hall to where Janey was waiting impatiently by the door. Janey was all that had kept her going since those forty-eight hours had elapsed: her happiness had been the driving force which had stopped her from breaking down completely and giving in to this grief that was slowly tearing her apart. Now she fixed a smile to her face for the benefit of her daughter.

'Right, then, where to today?'

'Swings!' Janey laughed happily, untouched by the trauma as she hopped excitedly from one foot to the other.

Maggie smiled sadly as she took her hand and they started along the road to the park. It was a kind of sweet pain to look at the little girl now because she reminded her so vividly of Matthew. He should have been here to share things like this walk to the park with them, but her actions of three years ago, her inability to handle the situation in an adult manner, had denied them both that right.

The park was nearly deserted at this time of the day and Maggie took her time, stopping frequently while Janey picked up leaves and other little treasures to show them to her. Reaching the playground, she lifted the child into one of the baby swings and fastened the straps securely across her lap, then started to push her gently.

'More, Mummy, more!' Janey squealed her delight, kicking her feet as the swing arced towards the sky, and Maggie felt tears of regret for what she'd done sting her eyes. Fumbling in her pocket, she found a tissue to wipe them away then murmured crossly when the wind blew it from her hand. She bent down to pick it up then started nervously when a pair of long jeans-clad legs suddenly came into view and a deep voice said softly, 'Hello, Maggie.'

She straightened abruptly, the blood thundering along her veins, wiping away her ability to even think.

'Careful!'

He pulled her away from the swing as it dropped back again, moving her easily to one side before taking her place, his hands sure and steady as he assumed the task of pushing the child. Maggie drew in a shaky breath, staring at him as though he were a ghost, and he smiled crookedly.

'You did say to come,' he taunted gently, a wealth of meaning in his tone so that she blushed.

'I... What took you so long?' She didn't mean to sound so snappy and churlish, but his unexpected appearance had knocked her completely off balance. She had mentally prepared herself for this meeting, imagined how it would be and what she would say, but it had always been on her terms with her totally in command. How typically perverse of Matthew to surprise her like this!

He leant a shoulder against the metal support while he pushed Janey back and forth as though it was the most natural thing in the world for him to do. 'I had a few things to clear up before I could take you up on your invitation. I hope I've not left it too late?'

He raised a mocking brow, amusement written all over his infuriating, impossibly handsome face, and Maggie ground her teeth.

'And what if I say that you have? Will it make any difference?'

He shook his head, his black hair falling over his forehead in a way that made her fingers itch to reach out and brush it back. 'Not a bit.'

'Then there doesn't seem much for me to say! Look, Matthew, I——'

'You...what? Surely you're not getting cold feet already, are you, Maggie? I thought you had more spunk in you than that.'

'No, I am not getting cold feet!' she snapped, stung into replying without a shred of caution.

'Good. That's what I hoped you would say.' He caught her hand and pulled her into his arms, his lips cold from the wind, yet not cold enough to disguise the fire she could feel burning just beneath the surface. Just for a moment she clung to him, her lips giving back everything he gave her, before slowly she drew herself from his arms.

'We have to talk, Matthew,' she said quietly, pushing the wind-blown length of her hair back from her face. 'I know what I said to you the other day and it still holds firm, but there is so much we need to talk about before we can go on.'

'I know. But not just yet.' He looked at Janey, who was still happily swinging, his expression softening in a way that brought a lump to Maggie's throat. 'I've a lot of catching up to do, and now seems like the perfect time to start.'

They stayed in the park until dusk started to fall, then made their way back along the quiet paths. When Matthew put his arm around her and pulled her close she let herself lean against him, revelling in the feel of his hard body against her own. Janey was worn out by all the fresh air and exercise, not to mention the excitement of all the attention Matthew gave her, so that she could barely keep her eyes open while she ate her supper.

Maggie carried her up to bed straight afterwards, forgoing the usual bathtime and settling for washing her face and hands before tucking her up in bed. When she went back downstairs again Matthew was sitting on the sofa, his eyes closed, his head comfortably settled against the cushions, looking so *right* that it struck her afresh how much she stood to lose if they couldn't work things out.

'Don't, Maggie. Don't keep torturing yourself like this. We'll sort everything out. Damn it, we have to!'

There was a steely note in his deep voice as he sat up and glared almost fiercely at her, and she shuddered in sudden fear as the memories came rushing back.

'Can we? Just by sitting down and talking? We couldn't do it three years ago, so how are you so sure that we can do it now?'

'Because we're different people than we were then and we have so much more to lose.' He held her gaze. 'We have a child now. Surely her welfare must be uppermost in our minds?'

'Of course it must. But I can't help remembering how it was... all those bitter arguments. I don't think I can go through that again.'

'People always argue, Maggie. You can't live with someone and expect it always to be total harmony. That's unrealistic.' He stood up, pacing the floor. 'You were always so afraid of arguing a point out into the open, but why? It didn't mean that I loved you less because I disagreed with you.'

'I...' She cast her mind back, forcing herself to see what had prompted her fear of dissent. 'It just didn't seem right. People in love don't argue all the time!'

'We never argued all the time. You have it all out of perspective. Yes, we had disagreements, but that was only natural when we were trying to get to know one another. You had a totally unrealistic view of what married life should be like!'

Had she? Maybe he was right. She'd had such little experience of home life outside the confines of the children's home where she'd been brought up. A shy, withdrawn child, she had hated the rough and tumble of life there and painted pictures in her head of what a *real* home should be like, an idealised world where nothing unpleasant like arguments ever happened. She had been unprepared for the truth of how difficult it could be for two people to live together and build themselves a close relationship.

'You tried too hard to placate me when what you should have done was stand up for yourself.' He smiled harshly. 'I'm not proud of how I behaved, but it owed a lot to the way I too was brought up, expecting other people to always fall in line with what I wanted. The more you gave, the more I took.'

'But it wasn't just that.' She swallowed hard, hating what she had to say in case it destroyed this tentative understanding. 'You were so jealous, Matthew! The things you said, what you accused me of...'

There was pain in her voice and his face tightened. Just for a moment he seemed to make a move towards her, before stopping abruptly as though he knew this wasn't the time to touch her. 'I was frightened as well, Maggie. Frightened of losing you, frightened of the power you had over me. All my life my father had drummed it into my head that love was a weakness no man could afford to indulge, and I had lived by that code, taking what I wanted from women without any of them touching me inside. Then I met you and there I was, head over heels in love with you, and there wasn't a thing I could do about it!' He laughed shortly. 'It tore me apart to see you with other men, to see how natural you were, laughing and joking, when you were always so on edge with me. I'd walk into a room and watch you smiling at someone, and then you would turn and see me and all that brightness would fade. It hurt, Maggie...it hurt one hell of a lot!'

'I didn't know.' Her voice was very soft, soothing, as though she were speaking to a small child rather than this strong independent man who had always seemed so invulnerable. 'I could laugh and joke with others because they meant nothing to me. You were all that was important to me yet, no matter how hard I tried to convince you of that fact, I couldn't seem to make you believe it.'

'And David?' There was a wealth of self-disgust on his face as he asked the question. 'I have to know what your relationship was with him.'

She took his hand, holding it between both of hers. 'David was my friend. He helped me when there was no one else in the world to turn to. Maybe some day he will be that again. I don't know. But I was never in love with him, nor did we ever share an intimate relationship.' She met his eyes steadily. 'The only man I have ever slept with is you, Matthew, for the simple reason that you are the only man I have ever wanted. When you found me at David's flat that day, in his bed, it was simply because I had been taken ill on my way home from the doctor's after having my pregnancy confirmed. I was carrying your child then, Matthew, and the last thing on my mind was another man!'

'Why didn't you tell me?' His fingers clamped around hers, hurting her in his pain at the disclosure.

'Because I was afraid that you wouldn't believe that the baby was yours. You were so blinded by jealousy that day that can you honestly say that you would have accepted my word that you were the father?'

'I don't know! I was so devastated by what I thought was going on between you both that I don't think I will ever know the answer to that.' Suddenly all the anger drained out of him, leaving his face grey. 'It cuts me up to think what you went through, having our child all by yourself. Would you have ever told me the truth if it hadn't been for that kidnapping?'

She hated what she had done to him, hated to see the defeat on his face. 'Yes, I would have told you. I had already realised what a mistake I'd made by keeping it from you, but I just couldn't seem to find the right moment to tell you when all we did was argue when we met.'

'Well, that's something, I guess.' He let her hands go, moving deliberately away from her as though he wanted to give her some space. 'So where do we go from here?'

'Where do you want to go? You might be a few days late, but you did come, Matthew!'

There was a trace of dry humour in her voice, and something flashed in his eyes in quick response.

'I did indeed. But I have to warn you, Maggie, that circumstances have changed.'

'In what way?'

'In the fact that I might very well find myself out of a job if the police go ahead and prosecute me for handing over those papers, not to mention all the unsavoury publicity when the trial restarts and all the details come out.'

'Surely you must have explained what happened? Damn it, I shall tell them myself if you won't!'

'And this is the lady who says she doesn't like arguments?' He laughed softly as he linked his hands behind her waist. 'I've told them everything, Maggie. That's what I've been doing all week and why I didn't come to you sooner. I've been trying to sort the whole mess out.'

'And what do you think will happen?'

He shrugged, his hands smoothing down over the soft curve of her hips as he eased her closer. 'They have been surprisingly sympathetic, so hopefully I will just get a strong reprimand and that will be that. If not, well...'

'If not then we shall have to face it together, won't we?' She raised herself on tiptoe to brush his mouth with hers, then drew back, enjoying the way he shuddered in betraying response.

'Witch!' he accused tautly, pulling her so close that she was left in little doubt of how he felt.

'Tut, tut, is that any way to speak to the mother of your child?'

His eyes darkened and he bent his head to nip gently at the delicate cords of her neck, making her shudder just as he had done. '*Our* child seems to have the right idea, so why don't we follow her example and go to bed?'

'Are you worn out by all the fresh air too?' Her eyes widened in mocking question before she gasped as he swung her up into his arms.

'I'm not worn out yet, but I have every intention of being so before the night's through!'

They made love slowly, the light from the moon filtering in through the parted curtains to frost their bodies with an ethereal, silvery light. Matthew took his time undressing her, his hands and lips smoothing time and again over her body in a silent loving homage which brought tears to her eyes.

Never had they loved like this before with this depth and intensity, this total harmony, as though their souls were linked on some magical plane. Each slow caress, each sweet lingering kiss was a heady torment as he brought her to the very brink of passion, then paused.

'I love you, Maggie. I never stopped loving you and I never shall.'

'And I love you, Matthew.'

The words whispered from her as he slid down and took her in a wild frenzy of passion which tipped her over the very edge of control, echoing inside her head again and again like a talisman for the future.

She repeated them later when they lay side by side, her head cradled on his shoulder, enjoying the fact that she could finally say them aloud without fear but with joy in her heart.

'I love you, Matthew.'

He drew her closer into his arms, his body curving protectively around hers as they drifted off to sleep, to be awakened hours later by Janey's arrival in the room.

Maggie blinked the sleep from her eyes, pushing herself up on the pillow as she watched the surprise on the child's face when she suddenly realised that Matthew was in the bed. She hesitated uncertainly, watching as Matthew rolled over and sat up.

'I think there's just about room for a little girl in here, don't you, Maggie?'

Maggie smiled her relief at his easy understanding of the situation, feeling the last of her re-
servations fade away. Leaning over, she kissed him
quickly, then gasped when a small whirlwind hurled
itself on to the bed and pushed between them.

'And me.' Janey planted an enthusiastic kiss on
Maggie's cheek before turning shyly towards
Matthew, obviously unsure whether to afford him
the same treatment.

Maggie slid her arm around her daughter, looking
over her head to meet his eyes as she said softly,
'Give Daddy a kiss, darling.'

Next Month's Romances

Each month you can choose from a world of variety in romance with Mills & Boon. Below are the new titles to look out for next month, why not ask either Mills & Boon Reader Service or your Newsagent to reserve you a copy of the titles you want to buy — just tick the titles you would like to order and either post to Reader Service or take it to any Newsagent and ask them to order your books.

Please save me the following titles:	Please tick	√
A HONEYED SEDUCTION	Diana Hamilton	
PASSIONATE POSSESSION	Penny Jordan	
MOTHER OF THE BRIDE	Carole Mortimer	
DARK ILLUSION	Patricia Wilson	
FATE OF HAPPINESS	Emma Richmond	
THE ALPHA MAN	Kay Thorpe	
HUNGARIAN RHAPSODY (This book is free with THE ALPHA MAN)	Jessica Steele	
NOTHING LESS THAN LOVE	Vanessa Grant	
LOVE'S VENDETTA	Stephanie Howard	
CALL UP THE WIND	Anne McAllister	
TOUCH OF FIRE	Joanna Neil	
TOMORROW'S HARVEST	Alison York	
THE STOLEN HEART	Amanda Browning	
NO MISTAKING LOVE	Jessica Hart	
THE BEGINNING OF THE AFFAIR	Marjorie Lewty	
CAUSE FOR LOVE	Kerry Allyne	
RAPTURE IN THE SANDS	Sandra Marton	

If you would like to order these books from Mills & Boon Reader Service please send £1.70 per title to: Mills & Boon Reader Service, P.O. Box 236, Croydon, Surrey, CR9 3RU and quote your Subscriber No:..(If applicable) and complete the name and address details below. Alternatively, these books are available from many local Newsagents including W.H.Smith, J.Menzies, Martins and other paperback stockists from 11th September 1992.

Name:..

Address:...

....Post Code:......................

To Retailer: If you would like to stock M&B books please contact your regular book/magazine wholesaler for details.

You may be mailed with offers from other reputable companies as a result of this application. If you would rather not take advantage of these opportunities please tick box ☐